MW00633495

UNREQUITED LOVE

By

Gayle DeGuzman

To Theresa,
Enjoy
GDeGuzman

Dedication

Lovingly dedicated

to my family, friends and readers.
Life is to be enjoyed to make it worth living!

Special mention to
Luke, my staunch Sr. Publisher
Zack, most understanding Project Manager
And to my Editors of BWB
Thank you very much!

About the Author

Gayle DeGuzman is a woman full of passion with far reaching interest, experience and calling, with degrees in Associate of Arts and a Bachelor of Arts from Universities and certificates from various seminars of governmental agencies. She held licenses to practice Real Estate, Nurse Assistant and a diploma in Computer Programming. Her professional achievements are due to her perseverance and dedication to every venture she dared to accomplish. Having worked in different fields; banking for 17 years, realty, medical, data processing and estate administration, her novels reflect her expertise and knowledge of things she wrote about.

She values people from all walks of life having been a customer and service-oriented person all her life. She loved sailing in their McGregor catamaran as well as working on her other hobbies of quilting, knitting and gardening. Continuing education and reading all kinds of books are her ways to amass knowledge to fully understand and appreciate our ever-changing world.

Her writings portray love as the greatest emotion encompassing all shades of humanity. Her three published books, 'After All These Years' is a story of love, fortitude and triumph while 'Love Beckons' is about faith and hope, and 'Unrequited Love,' all touching on exemplary virtues to surmount frailties. She has written other eleven (11) books, coming out soon, all sizzling about love and values! Her stories are full of laughter, wits and exciting exchanges of interesting characters that make every reading experience a pleasure!

She's enjoying life to the fullest, never in vain as she has conquered all her life's inequities, happy her children are living their best. She now lives in the beautiful Vancouver Island in Canada, in the Pacific Northwest!

Table of Contents

Part #1

To a man who broke a woman's heart, he would not be the last she would ever love in her lifetime!

"Better to have loved and lost than never to have loved at all."

"A real man never hurts a woman. Be careful when you make her cry because God counts her tears. The woman, created by God, came out from a man's rib, not from his feet to be walked on, and not from his head to be superior, but from his side to be equal, under his arm to be protected, and next to his heart to be loved." A very wise quote!

Hurt from a love spurned, it was the emotion felt from unrequited love! Always quoted wisely by older people than younger ones who had felt the hurt and the pain of the loss! Some would never love again! Others would find love again! Truly, there was no retreat from love; should the right one come along, good luck prevailed!

There was hope for as long as one would ever live; there would always be someone to have, to hold, and to love. Love is the greatest feeling one could ever have for someone who could set her feelings on fire, her desire to long for ecstasy, and her eyes for him only. Her commitment to wait for the day she could say her vows- to love and to cherish until death do us part- was the lure, love's greatest promise!

But at times, love could be painful, hurtful and the loss meant indescribable suffering for the one who was left behind either by death or willful, bitter desertion. Due to the insurmountable grief and pain of anguish and the belief that no one could ever again feel the magic of love, one never tried to love again, for it made life more bearable just living in the realm of bygone memories of the lost love.

How love could make Jasmine's heart whole again was at odds with the likelihood of finding someone she could trust to restore the kind of affection and respect she wanted in her life. To her, men were all alike- no exception! She would not allow a different perspective to pull her in a different direction, deluded to think she had anchored herself to the solid ground of complacency and could forever hold on tight, never again succumb to another man's charm.

Until then, the force and magic of love working in tandem could not be taken for granted or underestimated by any means, like a twinkle of the eye, a fleeting glance, a burst of laughter, or a nice tender gesture, such could play havoc to a frail heart, and voila! Love could be born in an instant when least expected! There was no refuge from love! Love's smoldering embers could ignite the dissipating glow to give that warm feeling that was fast to envelop the heart, titillate the emotion, and enslave one's disposition. One could hardly say no, or refuse kindness but is swayed to follow the flow! Soon, confusion between pleasantness and love would come into play, rendering one helpless but to follow what the heart dictated. Did anyone, whoever fell in love, know what hit them hard? Love, they said, was merrier the second time around! Much sweeter and intoxicating if allowed to grow and flourish!

It was a fine day. Jasmine was in contemplation, filled with eagerness- working on her chores, when a little jazzy, good-listening music started playing on her recorder in the background, stirring memories of yesteryears. Her life was not really that lonely; she had it under control. She had learned to set aside the unpleasant and kept herself preoccupied with work and hobbies, like knitting, quilting, gardening, and creative writing, to name a few.

At night, after watching TV news, she would spend the night with her quilts. If the mood struck to write, she would spend hours and hours on creative writing- writing short stories or finishing her novel, with soft background music adding tranquility to the atmosphere, with her mind inducing ideas and aspirations conducive to good storytelling. Her work area next to her room was functionally built to suit her working needs, a computer area where she would do her writing, communicate with friends and relations, and a small library of books, on science, documentary, and fiction for her reading pleasure, her personal files, all set and well organized for easy access. Her work center was divided by a glowing fireplace, double-faced, one facing the front room and the other facing her work room, considered very energy efficient and inexpensive, considering that she was comfortably living on a single income! On one side of the room was a record player with her collection of CDs on music and movies, sewing and quilting tutorials, while on the other half center was her quilting tables, cutting and assembling area with lots of drawers and cabinets full of clothing materials, threads and miscellaneous items for sewing, even painting. Nearby, a den had a wide couch and a loveseat placed on both sides of the room to make good relaxation possible after a hard day's work. A good-sized comfortable bathroom was functionally built with a second door to access her adjoining bedroom, so she could quickly go back and forth when working late at night. She designed a safety feature to make her fully shielded from would-be intruders and for good privacy!

Her phone rang. Suzy, very energetic, was on the line, "Hey you, remember Mario from ADP, the one who had a headhunter friend?" Suzy, her officemate and friend, was calling to give her information on a new data processing company hiring new employees, knowing that Jasmine was not happy with her present position at her workplace. Even though she would miss her company, it was important that she was happy at work, so she told a friend about it and now got some feedback that could be useful to Jasmine.

"Yeah, I remember Mario. You mean he knows someone and can help me get employed at that Computing outfit? Tell him to call me, and I'll try to make an appointment with him. That's nice for a change of environment, I'm getting depressed by the day, and I can't keep going anymore. I need to make a good living with my mounting expenses and new lifestyle! Thank you, Sue, you're a real darling. I'll keep you posted." After saying goodbye to Suzy, she sat there thinking, *"wouldn't that be nice- get a new job, earn good money and keep moving on?"* She wanted a new life with new hope, leaving her frustrations behind.

After a week of talks and appointments, Jasmine was hired. She had complied with a notice given to her former employer and was to report to the new place on the first of the following month. Suzy threw out a going-away party for her with a few friends. She felt happy to move on despite the glumness in leaving nice people behind, especially Suzy, but knew their friendship would go on! One more plus about the new employment was the elimination of traveling in heavy traffic. The new office was nearer her home, and the privileges were great, a step up in the right direction, managerial level for her chosen career in computer science. It was a bigger company and had branches all over the country.

She was getting accustomed to her responsibilities when the accounting department manager gave her a memo about a seminar in Las Vegas for the weekend she had to attend. It was mandatory, especially for a new hire.

"Ready for Vegas this weekend? After that, we're in for another adjustment, major shuffling of VIPs from one branch to another," one supervisor told her. "Let's keep our fingers crossed not to be under an arrogant AVP! By the time we're back from Las Vegas, the new AVPs should have met everyone except us! That's quite a dramatic entrance for us!" They all laughed at the joke!

"Sure, let's have fun and worry later about new Department Heads. It happens all the time; just hope for the best and not get under those strict 'know it all' and obnoxious kinds." They laughed about that too!

The weekend was great. The seminar was fun and informational, and it gave Jasmine a new perspective on life, which was perfect for her dwindling attitude. She would settle down well with this new job, and then there would be no reason why she would look for another place of work ever again! She liked her office very much. Situated on the third floor of the building, facing the view of the oceanfront and on the same floor with the various department heads. It was just one floor above the cafeteria and the Computer room, which she knew would be the places she'd frequent the most to submit job runs and spend some time for coffee while waiting for her preliminary output.

She had just been working there a month and really did not care who the new department head would be until probably later in the shuffle. In the meantime, she was coordinating efficiently with the accounting department and the accounts department for newly acquired clients. She knew that the new head of Quality Control had already met all the personnel except her because she was away on a seminar. She had forgotten that she had to meet the boss when Marie showed up; she was to usher her to the AVP office, just across from hers, a few doors to the north side of the building by the elevator. As seen from the stairway, a good-sized balcony, covered with enormous landscape plants to provide shade and privacy, was facing the length of the coastline view. Those amenities were available to the company executives only!

Marie, the executive secretary, knocked, opened the door, and showed her in to meet her new boss. As the door behind her closed, she curiously approached the desk of a light brown-haired, very tall, impeccably dressed gentleman who was busy looking at a folder on the opposite counter by the window, then turned around to look at her. She was astounded as he was that she dropped her folder! He was as stunned and speechless at her sight after a long six years!

"I'm sorry, I think I'm in the wrong place." She said, gathering her papers, and then started to walk out of his office, trying her best to avoid looking at him.

"Stay, please, sit down," he ordered in a soft but commanding voice. She hesitantly complied. "You're in the right office, looking at your paperwork here, and you are under my department. I'm sorry, I'm as astonished as you are. But here we are, in the same place of work and would be working with each other."

She seated herself as ordered, but she did not say a word until he spoke again. "Aren't you glad we're able to see each other again, after several years of not knowing if we would ever meet again?"

Zachary Ray Jennings, the man she had tried very hard to forget and whom she wished to have never encountered again, was now standing in the flesh before her eyes, as commandingly attractive as she could remember, but now as her immediate boss, the department head, and AVP of the company she recently chose to work over others.

She was unable to fathom the right words to address her boss. She thought she was incapacitated and had lost her voice for a while. He looked at her, closely studying everything about her, absorbing her wholesome beauty, demurely seated in front of him, in his mind. He wondered how she had evolved to be as elegant and attractive as a woman now compared to the fiery, freckled impish girl she used to be. Jasmine was the only person he knew and cared about in his early days, the one he had held dear to his heart, but he left her in pursuit of a better future without saying a word of goodbye. How had he longed to see her! How long ago was it? Six years and counting! It was awesome to behold her beauty and wholesomeness again finally! However, the prolonged absence made them strangers to each other! Would he be able to bridge the gap?

"I'd like to put in my resignation. I'm sorry I can't work with you." She finally said, trying her best to compose her battered dignity that was again shattered by this man who thought so little of her. Having him once again in her life was an option she was not willing to take! She could not afford to see him on a daily basis! And as her boss to order her around and abide by his bidding? No way!

"Jazz, please."

"Don't call me that, please. You have no right to address me that way!"

He could not say a word to appease her infuriation at the moment. He stood up from his desk to sit on the chair fronting her. "Give me a chance, please! Can we start from the beginning? It does not have to be this way." His eyes were pleading for consideration. "Don't give up your chance of a good job on my account. This place of work is worth your while!"

Without looking at him, she focused her concentration on the folder she held. "I'm sorry, I don't need the tension of working with you, and with the stress of the job, I won't survive. I can't afford to lose my sanity ever again. I have other options."

Her words aptly described her disappointment in meeting him again. She did not want anything to do with him. Though it was a casual rejection, it was inconsiderate without giving him a chance! She was declining to work under him amid the tension and stressful balancing of accounts, especially on a monthly deadline of reports on computer runs, further complicated by her emotional distress. He understood why she was running away, in rejecting a good work opportunity as soon as he showed up as her immediate boss. The person who stood her up and discarded her without mercy and consideration, a shadow of her foreboding past who took away her dignity and harshly changed her attitude in life.

"I know how unpleasant everything is. I fully understand how you feel, but please give the job a chance. I promise to treat you with dignity and respect; I will try my best to be out of your way most of the time. I'll give you independence in your work and authorization on various accounts. Just provide me figures that I need to work on clients' requests, at the least. Other than that, all communication with me can go through the system. Please don't blow this up on me." Once more, he implored her as his life depended on her decision to work out things with him.

She did not respond- instead, she stood up and said, "I'll think about it. I was told there was a shuffle of Department Heads, the reason why probably you were assigned here, so it was not your fault. We both did not know that we would be paired together. No one from here knew me- I was recruited by a headhunter from a friend. If the relationship between us becomes untenable, I can always return to my former employer, who has offered me the option to rejoin the company."

"Thank you, Jasmine, I'll be greatly indebted to that decision, and I appreciate your candor. That's all for now, and welcome to the department. I'll see you tomorrow to work on a schedule with your preference if you already have one. Good day." He stood up and walked her to the door without extending his hand for a handshake in case she was still bent on a rebuke.

Zach went back to his desk, sat, and stared at the paperwork on Jasmine's employment, strained of energy but thankful he was able to talk her out of quitting and accept the proposition of working with him. He knew he had to work doubly hard to regain her trust and friendship. He knew these days were stressful, long, and taxing, but he was very confident about how hard-working, efficient and reliable she was, as long as he kept his distance! He would be walking on a fine line when working closely with her, especially on the mid and end of the month computer report runs.

He would deal with another blow if ever she discovered he had asked a headhunter to track her down and offered her a job in the company where he was a department head, not necessarily in the branch where he was. By that time, he would have probably won her trust and possibly her heart.

She did not have any more interaction with Zach other than a few emails from him about a new client's profile in which case, he scheduled a short meeting with the New

Accounts and Accounting reps at about 9:00 am the following day at his office, requesting her presence. Of course, she had to be there to make sure she knew their work schedule. She went home at precisely 6 pm, an hour past her time, but she preferred to go home late because she wanted to clear her desk and submit her run schedule to the computer room and inform her boss about it, in case he had another client's run request.

When she left, most of the offices had their lights on, including Zach's office, who was probably catching up with his workload. She hesitated before switching her lights off, closed her door, and hurriedly walked past his office to the elevator, afraid to be seen by Zach, not knowing how to react or what to say to him if they saw each other face to face. She knew it would be awkward for both of them and wished that the tension would disappear soon.

She walked faster as if someone was hot on her heels and was relieved when she had the car started and moving, driving out of the parking lot. She glanced at the space where it had a sign 'QC Department Head' and knew it was Zach's car, a gray BMW, next to hers- the Quality Control Manager. He had started a week ago, but she did not meet him until today, after the Vegas seminar. He was always out of his office meeting the top people in their branch- that was why he was unaware of her working under him until they met that day!

The meeting with the other department reps was vital to her work, whose input she had to include with her running schedule submitted to the computer room for time allocation. Zach was very professional in his work ethic and always referred to her with respect. He had a tinge of familiarity like an old co employee and friend, which made her loosen up her rigidity and relax at the end of the meeting. Some handshakes were exchanged by the others but not between her and Zach. She tried to leave hurriedly but halted at the door when Zach asked her to stay behind to discuss her revised work schedule further. She got a little nervous about being alone with him but went back to her seat after courteously helping Zach put back the other chairs over to one side of his office.

"As we had talked about your work scheduling, I get it, but I have a few suggestions here if you don't mind looking through them. I need your feedback." While Jasmine was looking through the paperwork, Zach had the chance to look at the new face across him, tracing back the familiarity he was used to. He had enjoyed gazing at her sweetness. He remembered calling her 'Jazz' or 'Freckles' and even 'Brown Eyes'- these were his favorite pet names for her, depending on his teasing mood. But now, she had made it clear that he was forbidden from calling her fondly! She wanted to be treated with formality and decorum, not as a close confidante anymore, for that woman had long been gone and was nowhere near the new Jasmine of today.

When it was Zach's turn to review the changes she made to the paperwork, she had the chance to fully gaze at Zach's face studying those familiar handsome planes and lines she dearly loved and admired. To her, Zach was the symbol of someone perfect and her one and only; that was why she could not reconcile the harshness he meted out when he decided to just go and throw away all their shared memories. Now she had to keep her distance and be cold and uncaring, just the opposite of what they used to be.

Zach put his initials on it and handed her the paperwork after a few other suggestions, she stood up, gave him a forced smile, and walked to the door. Zach, in return, stood up, gave her an approving nod, but waited for the door to close behind her. There was tension, but he knew, in his heart, that Jasmine was a cordial person, and soon she would find it in her heart to forgive him and maybe go back to where they were before, he prayed and hoped.

Jasmine was not happy with the way things were between her and Zach, but what else could she do? She couldn't find it in her heart to forget the bitterness and the pain inflicted on her by his total disregard for her feelings in the past. She had to stop dwelling on the hurt; she had to start living and believing there must be a good reason why her path had crossed with Zach's again. Or, start treating Zach like a stranger she just met in her new place of work, forget him as the person she had dearly loved before who later abandoned and hurt her. The latter option sounded better, treat Zach as a new person she just met, with fewer complications!

Again, she worked an hour past her time, did the routinary closing, and walked casually to the elevator without glancing at Zach's office. It was a step closer to her decision to change her work attitude, which was better with the stress of the work schedule and heavy client communication. She did not have to discuss anything with Zach as long as she worked within her authority scope. Even when walking to the parking lot, she was no longer in a hurry to jump into her car and drive away as fast as she could; she had managed to take her sweet time instead. She felt things were getting better every day as she got used to her work schedule, became familiar with her surroundings, and pushed Zach away from her consciousness, treating him like other QC employees around.

Zach noticed that Jasmine was more relaxed and was not as tense as she used to be when answering his inquiries on the phone intercom, sounding more confident, less hesitant, almost at ease, and friendly at times. He stayed well on his side of the bargain and kept his promise not to invade her working space unless urgent, tapped to get his information from other sources and be diplomatic with his request.

What Jasmine was afraid of was close contact with him, but he avoided that with his best efforts. She was aware of his ways of ignoring her when passing by his office and if they saw each other in the computer room or at the cafeteria, where they casually said 'hi' or talked a bit and moved on like it was customary. She knew he was getting settled and better with their daily routine and encounters. There was no hurry on his part, knowing she would eventually come around. Until then, Zach would hold his tongue, not to open up about their past, lest he'd be in trouble. Each working day was a new beginning.

One early morning, Jasmine was having a cup of coffee at a table next to the counter when Zach walked in and went directly to the dispenser. While getting a packet of sugar and a stirrer, he noticed her and said, "Good morning, Jasmine." She raised her cup to acknowledge his greetings. He approached her table and said, "Mind if I give this note to you here about Alaska?"

"Not at all. What's it about?" She said and gestured for him to sit, but he did not; instead, he handed her the note and waited for her to look at it. "As usual, they need a preliminary run. Sure, I'll talk to Steve in the computer room tonight." As soon as he got her response, he smiled, thanked her, and walked away with his cup of coffee, then stopped by another table and chatted with the other manager.

One time, in the computer room, Zach walked in to find Jasmine discussing a client's request for reports with Steve. He looked through his own department's schedule of work while Steve was busy with her, then approached them and turned to Jasmine as she started to walk away, "Jasmine, could I pass by your office for some notes about Investors'

Titles before Steve runs their reports tonight? I'm referring to their previous month's run if you could pull it up for me."

"Sure thing, it will be ready for you." She waved her hand to both of them and went out the door and back to her office. Lenny, her assistant, had left for her lunch break, so she was alone in the area. She went to her computer right away and pulled the requested information, ready for Zach when he came by. He knocked on the door twice, opened it, and promptly pulled a chair to view the account on the computer screen as casually as he could to dispel tension.

Like two people working cooperatively, the interaction was smooth, and no discomfort for both of them, as long as the subject was about work. While she was talking, explaining the information on the screen, he was attentively listening, jotting down notes. Every once in a while, he directed her to fish out other essential parameters that needed to get changed; therefore, he would have to notify the programmer to modify the application- make the necessary changes to facilitate QC to select the input choices to generate whatever request the client would have in the future.

"That's better for us. We can have a small run, save computer time and input the necessary parameters to generate a special report, instead of a costly run of the whole job." Jasmine said, indicating a request from the QC department was an excellent decision to save time and cost by including various parameters and the ability to select one for a particular report!

After their consensus on the job matter, Jasmine relaxed and looked at Zach, who felt a bit uncomfortable being that close to her, with their eyes locked in an unexpectedly tender moment. He stood up suddenly, not knowing how to curtail the momentary lapse of his promise not to invade her space. What was left for him was to give her a nonchalant smile and he later said, "Thank you, I'll talk to the programmer, and you can do the necessary change for this specific run." He then left as fast as possible to avoid betraying his raw emotions for her, now overwhelming him.

Zach was now beginning to realize the pain and the costly wedge of inconvenience between them. Jasmine knew what made him leave as fast as possible, and she could not blame him, but it left a bit of satisfaction to her. As days passed, her firm resolve was hardened, and her heart grew number- no longer obsessed by her past mistake of loving someone who did not love her in return, but a resolute purpose of forgetting was unwavering. She knew she could do it again, to survive and forget all about him. She had all her life to live and maybe someday all her love to give, should she find love again! But for now, she would not let Zach into her heart again, nor would she crave his attention.

Zach, day by day, noticed the changes in Jasmine, though subtle, nevertheless was alarming to him. She was more relaxed and unaffected, more considerate, accommodating, and working harder, at the same time getting easy going and quite appealing. He was affected by the new changes in Jasmine, who was evolving into a lovely and sensual, though feisty at times, no longer the bold and energetic imp she used to be. Instead of softening, she was getting harder and unrelenting. But Zach was still bewildered, aware of her chameleon spunkiness, worried about the widening gap between them.

After mowing his backyard at home on a Saturday weekend, he got a phone call from Charlie, who tracked down Jasmine for him. "Hey Charlie, man, where are you? How come you never got in touch with me after that hard work you did?"

"I talked to my headhunter friend, and he told me Jasmine was working at your company and that you were eventually transferred, paired with her. What could be more awesome and rewarding after all those gone by years, huh?" Charlie said, happy to have successfully reunited two lost souls for the sake of love. "So, how are you two getting along?"

"Well, thank you is not enough for what you have accomplished. I'm so happy she's nearby working with me, but she hasn't forgiven me, though. I don't know if she ever will, but I'm happy knowing I'm nearby if she needs me. That's more than enough for me, but still hoping that one day I would be able to melt her cold heart and be forgiven for having deserted her."

"I'm sure she would come to her senses and realize there are a few of your kind. Was she able to figure out how you suddenly paired together?"

"Nope, but I don't think that would matter now even if she learned the truth that I pulled a lot of strings just to be near her again. She's working contentedly, and I don't invade her space. I watch at a distance, making her look back at her own free will to compare the person I was before and my heretofore." Zach chuckled with that prediction.

"You're good, Zach. You have suffered and atoned for the mistakes of your youth. If you like, we can put in a word for you through Suzy, her close friend from her previous employer. I know her through another friend. Maybe I can stage a 'catch up' event and see what's cooking. I want things to work out for both of you."

"Charlie, you're truly a nice friend. Yeah, why not, but let me think about it; if we do this, it must be foolproof because I can't afford to alienate her again. Are you staying long enough or ready to leave at the drop of a hat?" Zach asked Charlie, who was always on the go, but never missed calling Zach to say 'hi' each time he was in town.

"I am working on a new deal, and if it works, I'll be here for a few years; after that, I'd really need to plant my roots and start thinking of raising a family. I'm getting to be an old bull."

"Same with me, but my luck has not stricken yet. Why don't you bring your friend tomorrow afternoon at about 5 pm for a barbecue here in my backyard? Is that too soon?"

"We'll be there with you. Good, I miss the camaraderie, bud! See you then, bye." Zach hung up, happy to hear from Charlie and eager to see him tomorrow and contemplate whatever he's planning to cook up for him and Jasmine.

Sunday at about 5 in the afternoon, Charlie stopped his car in front of Zach's house with a friend named Joven. They went to the backyard, where Julie prepared the table for them. The meat was ready to be thrown on the grill, and the guys started the way they preferred cooking their own. The drinks were in the cooler, soft drinks and beer altogether.

"Well, first, let me introduce my little sister here, Julie. She's still in school but pretty soon will be using the services of a headhunter as well if she does not want to work with me." He turned to Julie and said, "Julie, this is Charlie, who helped me find Jasmine, and this is his friend Joven." After the handshakes and small-talk, they started eating just like old friends do, enjoying the taste and texture of the barbecued meat and the refreshing coolness of the beer. It was good eating!

After a while, Zach explained his relationship with Julie- the little sister of one of his friends from New York who died of a malignant brain tumor a year ago. The incident left Julie an orphan with no known relatives to live with, so he informally adopted her and helped her with her schooling.

His colleagues mistook her for his fiancée because of their close relationship, but they did not bother to correct them. No harm done since both were not in any love entanglement, better for Julie so that no nonsense guy would bother her, and for Zach, at least the overzealous women were off-limits when they saw him with her. Besides, their friends knew the actual situation and were proud of Zach's kind heart, treating poor Julie as a younger sibling.

Charlie proposed to involve Suzy, Jasmine's close friend and confidante, to soften Jasmine's attitude towards Zach. Charlie suggested that Zach show the truth of his quest to find her and his involvement in recruiting her to work for his company in LA, a better and more prestigious one than where Jasmine worked. But he never intended to cramp her style nor invade her space. Transferring to the branch where Jasmine was employed was never planned. It happened because Zach was preferred to man the Quality Control Department, his specialty, by the top CEO of the company. Zach was not aware that Jasmine would be working with him until the day she showed up in his office for a briefing.

It was the truth, and Zach was already a bit tired of apologizing for his mistakes and was ready for anything or any 'come what may' happening in the company. He tried hard to keep his promise to Jasmine, so far never harassed or indulged in any kind of impropriety, and was prepared to accept the consequence if that was what poetic justice meant. He was just trying his best to right a wrong and desired to help Jasmine climb the ladder of success because of her expertise.

Charlie went ahead and involved Suzy, who was more understanding about the predicament looming over Zach's head. Charlie arranged an informal meeting between Suzy and Zach, whom she had known much about from stories she got from Jasmine. So, he was some kind of a lost soul in need of warmth from another friendly person close to Jasmine for acceptance and understanding. The meeting will be another barbecue party at Zach's on a Friday afternoon, which was a holiday.

Charlie arrived on time with Suzy and Joven. Zach introduced Julie to the new guests and later explained his circumstances. Suzy did not promise anything, but she said Jasmine's bitterness was deep-rooted because of her pain, and she had reconciled her life now with the past. They were all speculative and enthusiastic about a possible softening of Jasmine's resolve, even if not reconciliation with Zach, but at least acceptance and forgiveness- they knew that true love could find mysterious ways to mend and forgive.

She had to go out of town that Friday evening to visit her family. The following Monday, after the holiday, she was sent on an assignment out of town. She would be gone a week, and as soon as she was back, she had to work on some messy problem from their sister company in San Diego, so there was no time to see Jasmine, who also told her she was up to her throat with monthly reports and requested special runs. Hence, they decided to see each other the following month. The delay was not pleasant to Zach, but he said he would rather wait than see no resolution in the best possible way.

The usual was happening with Zach and Jasmine; both were on the opposite end of the stick. They remained distant, cold, and uncertain of the future. Zach was resigned to just work and did not bother about anything else, whether there was any change in Jasmine's attitude towards him or none at all. He stopped trying because each time he failed added more to his frustrations.

Zach called home, told Julie to dress up, and would take her out to eat at one of the best places in town to celebrate her successful transition to the fourth year in college. Jasmine was meeting a couple in the same restaurant to celebrate their first anniversary. On leave from the Navy, her friend's brother was tagging along. It was not a match-making expedition as she had joked about at the dinner. His presence completed a foursome since she did not have a date.

When Zach came in with Julie, they were directed to a table opposite where Jasmine was seated with the Navy guy. She looked up and saw Zach holding hands with Julie, taking off her shawl and placing it on the other chair. They looked happy, and Jasmine was surprised to see how young and breathtakingly beautiful she was, so angelic and innocent. Even though an age difference showed, Zach was commandingly handsome in his dark gray shirt, silver tie, and lighter gray coat, and no one would say they were not equally matched. They looked like lovers enjoying a night out!

Jasmine concentrated on the menu and prevented herself from looking in Zach's direction. She hardly wanted to admit that she had lost her appetite and had dampened her enthusiasm to make her evening as enjoyable as meeting a new acquaintance, a tall Navy Officer, gorgeous in his uniform as should be. They were seated at a corner table where the lights were dimmer. A bushy decorative plant was providing privacy, like if they were on a date, not wanting anyone to recognize their identities, which she was very glad about. At least, Zach would not notice her.

Zach and Julie left earlier, Julie holding on to the crook of Zach's arm and his hand was on her tiny shoulders. She was about five foot seven with her heels to Zach's six-foot-two height. She looked very young, maybe not even quite eighteen yet, just about the age to start dating. She had heard rumors that Zach was engaged to her live-in girl; could that be the girl he was betrothed to? She knew Zach's family and close friends, and that girl was not related to him.

Jasmine was early at the office that Monday morning but was surprised to see Zach's car. It seemed he had beaten her to the early chores again. She passed by the computer room before heading to her office, and there he found Zach talking to Steve.

"Good morning, guys. Do we have any throwaways?" She approached them and checked what it was that kept them very engrossed. He looked at her, but she avoided looking back. He could not comment on her working too hard, coming way too early, and going home late at night. She did not believe in the so-called constructive criticism; everything was direct criticism; that was how she had grown to be so defensive. Zach seemed to have reached a point where it was useless to say anything, so he preferred to say nothing at all, just to be on the safe side of any argument.

"Jasmine, hey, I saw you at the Seafood Galore last Saturday night! Who was that gorgeous Navy guy with you on a foursome date, huh?" Chelsea, the lady supervisor at the Accounting department, said, then turned to Zach and told him, "And you, Zach, were as gorgeous and good looking with that young, angelic socialite you were with. I said to myself I should keep going to that place. I love the romantic ambiance; that way, I could find out all who your dates are."

"You were there?" In unison, Zach and Jasmine asked Chelsea, then looked at each other. Zach was dismayed to hear about a gorgeous guy with her.

"Yeah, that's why you can't deny who your dates were. Zach, she was gorgeous but looked very young. Are you a cradle snatcher?" Then turned to Jasmine, saying, "I thought you were not dating. Why become a spinster when that tall, handsome, gorgeous guy was all over you?"

"Mind your own business, Chelsea! It was an innocent dinner with my friends who were celebrating their first anniversary. Her baby brother was visiting them, nothing serious- just a casual dinner," Jasmine said, then rushed out of the computer room without looking at Zach. She went to the powder room to freshen herself up from the onslaught of Chelsea for making it known to Zach that she was dating a gorgeous Navy guy; her trying to hide the fact was now futile.

She was confused, though. She couldn't figure out whether she was angry about Zach dating a beautiful young woman or Chelsea announcing that she was out dating and enjoying herself. When she came out, she bumped into Zach, who looked displeased and somewhat perturbed by the revelation. She was unsure if she said she was sorry or heard him say so. She hurriedly went inside her office, worked as hard as she could, and hoped not to bump into Zach again. She went home much later than Zach because his office was dark when she left, but his car was still there when she reached the parking lot. Where could he have gone?

"Wondering where I am? Whether back in the arms of the angelic woman I took dining out?" Zach said with crisp sarcasm in his husky voice.

"It's none of my business. You need not explain, and it's nobody's business to question anyone who they are with.

Chelsea just takes everything as a joke. Don't mind her. It was an unfortunate incident; let's forget all about it and move on." Jasmine said without engaging her eyes on him but concentrated on her bunch of keys.

"No, Jasmine. We have to be adults here; once and for all, we need to sit down and come to terms. I find it unbearable that the two of us can't find common ground to bury the hatchet and start anew." He approached her, put out his hand, and said, "Hi, my name is Zachary Ray Jennings. I would very much like to make your acquaintance." He was grave-looking, waiting for her hand.

"Jasmine Jade Warloffe, pleased to meet you, Zachary." She said with a smile and gave her hand to shake his.

"The pleasure is mine, Jasmine." He laughed with a chuckle, pulled her hand close to him, gave her a bear hug, and whispered. "Thank you. I can sleep well tonight."

"That's good! You're welcome, Zach. Good night." And she opened her car door, and Zach moved away to allow her to get into her car. She opened her window and waved goodbye.

"Drive carefully; see you tomorrow. Bye." He said to her and smiled, happily waving his hand. For once, he was able to break the ice between them.

It was a reckoning for the two of them. They maintained distance, even though the ghosts of their past were gone, and the walls between them came down- innate goodness wiping away all traces of animosity. A new kind of tenderness was slowly evolving between them. They started being considerate of each other but worked hard and observed rules that were not forced on them but had done so to find peace in their newfound friendship.

Zachary Ray Jennings was back in business, back in good grace with Jasmine, his friend from yesteryears. After six years of separation, they came to work together and reconciled all their differences. The days were more fruitful and enjoyable, and both of them had nothing to worry about in their sad past.

"Hey, you, good morning! Want some muffins? Let's go have some coffee before working too hard." Zach, all smiles in Jasmine's office, inviting her to go for some coffee at the cafeteria.

"Good morning!" she greeted back, chirpily. "Sure, why not?" She left her desk and followed Zach for their morning break. "What kind did you buy?"

"Your favorite, of course, glazed apple. What else?" He gave her the small bag and shoved her slightly, looking happily at her beautiful smile. On their way to the area, they met Chelsea by the door, smiling about their new happy disposition.

"Nice to see you guys with your morning smile. It's such a lovely day!" And she gave them a toast from her own coffee mug as she continued on her way.

"She's just a happy person who goes with the flow- you can't afford to get angry with her natural ways. She thinks everyone is always in a happy mood like her." Jasmine commented on Chelsea's attitude, neither being critical nor judgmental.

"You're right. I can't see any reason to dislike her; she kids a lot," Zach cut in.

Jasmine was in a trance-like stance at home that evening when the phone rang, "Hey you, what's cooking? Can I come over? I'll bring Chinese noodles and finger food- I know you like Siopao." Zach was at the other end, enthusiastic as ever with that smiling, teasing voice that Jasmine remembered so well that the conversation sent a tickle to her achy heart.

"Say yes, gorgeous!" He added in wait, hoping Jasmine would agree. She would refuse to socialize most of the time, which alarmed Zach. He was becoming concerned about Jasmine's attitude nowadays, showing a melancholy attitude, and most of the time distant, unlike the fiery person she used to be. He was sure it was not about work; she worked efficiently. He wanted to know what was bothering her, and she had not confided in him. Could it be she was realizing how lonely life would be alone without a man in her life?

Zach, somehow, his life status was now different from what it used to be, but more than anything else, he wished to be back to his former life with Jasmine. Yet he knew that life went on- time waited for no one, and neither could anyone turn back the hands of time. Zach and a few of his classmates, including Jasmine, were buddies in high school. They were inseparable, especially during school activities. They were all sports-minded, playing basketball, baseball, and football, and Jasmine was the steady cheering fan! Zach was always preoccupied with his games, and unlike the other guys, he was not interested in pursuing any of the younger girls. He was satisfied with his friendship with Jasmine, whom he considered very attractive, pretty, and sexy! He knew, in his heart, that she was the one for him! However, that dream in his heart never came to realization when his family moved to New York. As time flew by, new goals came up, dreams changed, and so did Zach's pursuit of life.

Jasmine's voice disrupted Zach's reminiscence. "What are you up to, Zach? You know I need my peace and quiet. Just tell me what this is all about, and I can deal with it over the phone." She said lamely. She did not want to be alone with Zach, but she knew that Zach's determination could not be dampened when he aimed for something. Maybe, if she could feign feeling under the weather, Zach would skip the idea of coming over to see her. "I'm not really feeling well. I should, maybe, catch up on my sleep and rest. I also need to catch up on personal matters, which I've been ignoring for a while now."

"Jazz, please, stop with the excuses! Let me see you, it's important, and we can't resolve anything over the phone; I'll be quick, I promise. Besides, the wonton soup will be good for your dwindling attitude in life. You will thank me and be on your feet and happy again." Zach implored her with that sweet-sounding hiss in his voice. Jasmine knew that Zach would not take no for an answer and would be at her doorstep in no time, so it was better to accept the inevitable. That way, she could estimate the time of his visit and prepare herself for whatever Zach wanted to talk about. It was nice that Zach was back in her life again, but she felt something was still missing, and she could not exactly pinpoint what was pulling her down.

"Well, what can I do to stop you? Practically nothing! What you want, you always get! Okay, be here *pronto!* I'll be ready with whatever monkey business you have. See you." Her exasperation was evident but was still very sweet and appealing to Zach. It reminded him of the old days. It was like magic to his ears, to his mind and heart. He couldn't help but blame himself for losing the right to hold her in his arms, whisper longings and desires, and promise happiness and joy in her life. He knew he was one of the reasons why Jasmine was losing hope in life, her growing indifference, and her antisocial attitude.

He had left her without saying goodbye- no communication for five years in New York and another year even when he was back in California. He stayed away until he decided to find her through a headhunter, offering her a job with his company. He felt a bit vindicated when Jasmine accepted the offer, and she started working with the company, not knowing about his connection to it.

He was already living with Julie, never telling Jasmine about his circumstances in life, which came in bits and pieces, one by one, put together and later accepted as the status quo of his life. Zach, at no point in their renewed acquaintance, offered Jasmine any explanation, even about his regrets. Until recently, his personal interaction with Jasmine, seeing her at work daily- resurrected his repressed feelings for her. The inevitable later hit him like a boulder bigger than life that crushed him mentally and spiritually. It came to him latently, maybe due to his commitment to Julie, who was still in her senior college year before venturing into her chosen field, she was his responsibility, and there was no way out.

Jasmine showed no regret in letting him back into her life once again. If ever she was badly hurt then, now she had become numb and just treated each day as a new beginning, hoping that someday she could wipe out every fiber of him and his memory from her heart and mind when she could fall in love again. Although she felt joy and pain each time she saw him at the office, it kind of became a ritual of the desire and longing for him, followed by a sense of rejection.

Greeting him with a wholesome smile to look at and getting a warm welcome with a light hug from Zach made it worthwhile. They both felt good- the chemistry was obvious and undeniable, like two souls thirsting for each other, wanting to be in a warm touch, caressing closeness. Still, the thought that Zach was no longer free to do that anymore, being with Julie, made Jasmine sad! "Hi, how are you, Zach? What brought this rare visit? No matter, it's good to see you here, in my humble place! Come on in."

"Is this the storyteller talking, or my dearest lost friend?" Zach said softly, without letting go of the warm embrace easily. Still holding her, he extended his arms to look at Jasmine's eyes to see what he could read from them. He knew the loneliness, the haggard and weakening resolve that was trying to take over her personality. She was more serious looking now than she used to be in the earlier days. He let go and said, "Here, I brought you wonton soup to cure that malingering feeling and finger food to spruce up your waning attitude in life. Come out of it, Jazz. Life is still worth living, just give it a chance, and you'll be able to find happiness again." Zach knew he needed to keep encouraging her to stay positive in her perspective in life. "I'm aware of the unhappy gap in our lives; I didn't mean to move away and leave without saying goodbye. My one regret in life is not confronting my fears and confusion. It is never too late to apologize, Jazz. Please forgive me for the way I acted before up to now. Every time I think about you, every time I see you, that regret creeps up in my mind and heart. I was a fool for the decisions I made in my life. There is no one to blame except myself. Please, Jazz, I need you to understand and let go of the hurt I inflicted on you- on us. What 'might have been' is now far from our reach; it's gone, it's in the past, and we have no power to undo that. What we can do is accept and be resolute about what the future holds for us. We need to move on!"

"Is this the reason you came to me, now? About our past? I have forgiven what you did a long time ago for the misery of not knowing why you left without a word. I have learned to live my life by myself- I'm not dependent on anyone for guidance and influence. I've learned how to be happy with who I am. I don't need anyone anymore- I don't trust anyone enough to let them influence and control my life as you did once. Now, I don't need help from you in that department, Zach." She was looking straight at those blue eyes without a wink or displaying any weakness but showed courage in her mellowed brown eyes. She had the ability to make a strong resolve if ever she needed to.

"Thank you for that. I really appreciate the inherent goodness of your heart, the straightforward attitude, and the undiluted kindness you always give out to me. You're one extraordinary person worthy of respect and praise. I wish I could bring back the time, our time, but I'm helpless to that, Jazz. I know I'm responsible for another life and happiness, that of Julie, who has no fault in any of this. I need more time from you and your understanding. All I ask of you now is to allow me to help you in any way to make it right."

"There is nothing wrong to make right. I am who I am now, what I want to be, and through no fault of yours. There is no need to keep on apologizing about the past, what we have is now, what's here to stay, and nothing can ever change that! All we have to do is bury the past behind us and not resurrect it- not even a part of it! And you can go back to your Julie, own your life with her!" She looked straight into those blue eyes with her strong determination to quell the emotion of wanting him with a potent need that overruled every ounce of common sense she possessed. It took a lot of courage, almost driving her to the edge, to fight a sense of tenderness that kept tugging at her heart. As if the devil were on her heels, she dashed out to avoid the momentary insanity she was feeling. Zach was everything to her! No matter what she said or did otherwise!

It was a strong but lonely speech, and he wasn't buying it. She was someone who kept him on his toes, to loosen up with ease when caught in a tight situation, when he felt lost and adrift on unfamiliar ground. Zach found it difficult to get past personal resentment each time and wondered if he could get to be the old hat. Had they been lovers and were together day in and day out, would the fire burn off as quickly, or would the sight of her evoked fierce emotions, knocking the wind off him each time he laid his eyes on her? With her still out of his reach, a clear answer would never come by! His lips would never touch hers in a passionate, fiery shattering taking! How would he feel if a new lover kissed her sweet red lips? It, surely, would shatter his world!

She moved to the kitchen to set the plates for the food he brought. Zach went to follow her, his mind working, his heart beating faster, and he knew in his heart he still wanted her the way he did before. The reason he went away was that it was impossible to have her then- that's it. Badly, even if he knew he had buried the past, it had an uncanny way of resurfacing when he least expected it, like now, being overwhelmed with that hot desire, unappeased, throbbing, and wanting her desperately. She shot him a fleeting glance, a demure smile, but truly, underneath all that was a spine made of steel, a spunk with a spirit reaching out to his heart. All over again, his heart warmed, followed by regrets, wanting her like the air he needed to breathe in, to sustain life. But what about Julie? He can't abandon her right now. He needs more time.

"Thank you for the good food. It was nice of you to feed me like a starving orphan. Could we start talking about the business of why you came here tonight? It must be something important that you couldn't wait until tomorrow!"

"Don't mention it, you know I always love to come and just visit you every now and then, and I know the food you like! I don't really need a purpose to want to talk to you, but tonight I felt I couldn't set it aside any longer. Somehow I need to know how it would affect both of us."

"But tonight, what could be that some special thing to discuss that could have any possible effect on us, both?" She locked eyes with him, waiting for him to spill the beans. Zach was so handsome and very appealing; she would not mind getting closer to him like someone lost in the desert, thirsty for water, drawing him close to satisfy her thirst. But, she knew he would always belong to Julie, and she needed to stop daydreaming. She had no right to lust for his touch or kisses, lest she forgot her own bearing. It was always wonderful to be with him, to talk to him, despite the aftermath of gloom that enveloped her to subdue her emotions that could betray her feelings, exposing the lies that she was now living with, that she couldn't care less about him.

"I know I have no right to even ask, but I need to know from you, truthfully, how your life is. Is there someone in your life now worthy of your love?" He was thinking about the tall and handsome Navy guy Chelsea saw her with at the restaurant. He looked at her, his gaze very intense and searching. He did not know how he may be able to accept the truth or any consequential possibility of his suspicion.

Instead of anger or doubt, she was taken aback, instantly amazed by his sudden interest in her love life. Why did it matter, especially to him, whether she had found somebody new or not? After a momentary loss of common sense, she looked up with misty eyes and said, "You have no right to ask me that! You do not have to concern yourself with how my love life is coming along. It does not matter how I am living my life, whether in remorse or joy. But, thank you anyway. I also have a right to find happiness!"

"Jazz, you matter to me a lot, I may not have been vocal about my feelings before, but I know deep in your heart, you know me well, better than I know myself, for that matter. Everybody knows how much you mean to me, then and now. I want to know if you have found someone to take my place in your heart!" Zach was eyeing her carefully, trying to read her body language and whatever her soulful brown eyes were revealing, trying to communicate.

"If you knew how you felt about me, why in God's name did you not do anything about it? Instead, you punished me more than I could bear. And now you're telling me you care? It's way past the time, and to dwell on it would not right the wrong! It's adding insult to injury!" Jasmine's subdued sobbing did not go unnoticed- her tears fell and wetted her cheeks.

"Jazz, this is not right! I am sorry about adding more misery, but I really want to know where we both stand. I've been in great anxiety over it, not knowing if you still have feelings for me or not, and I have to know how you feel. I have to make a decision- an informed decision this time." He held out a tissue to her to dry her tears, then took her hand, and in heavy contemplation, he said, "I've been meaning to confront the reality between us, to find the right solution to, once and for all, do us justice."

Jasmine pulled her hand from his hold, could not bear the heat that seemed to scorch hers, hide her heart's desire and longings, lie once more about not wanting him, so he could make an honest woman of Julie, his responsibility now, his intended bride. That was what she knew from rumors. Was that the naked truth? She composed herself, and when she had steadied her voice, she said, "Zach, do not ever worry about me. I can handle it- I don't need your protection, the way I needed you when I was bullied by the boys. I'm now stronger and capable of making my own decisions, especially when it comes to relationships. I'm just taking my time, trying to live the rest of my unwedded life. No, there is no other one who owns my heart now, and you know it!" And she gave him a beguiling smile, seemingly innocent, and knew in her heart it was the truth!

"If you are telling me the truth, then I have to trust you, sans suspicions and doubts. I should be happy about the outcome of this talk. I'll expect you to be the same jolly person I used to hang out with. But I want you to never forget that I care a lot about you, you're as precious to me as the air I breathe every day, my dearest friend, always the sunshine of my life, and I'll be with you anytime you need me." He stood up and pulled her up close to him and whispered, "You'll always be the one for me, you're the one that got away in our past life, but I won't let that happen in our newfound world. You'll see, and you can count on that!" And he smiled and kissed the top of her head, sniffing the smell of lavender scent of her that he had always remembered. "Goodbye, sleep well. I'll see you tomorrow," he whispered again.

At that instance, Jasmine wanted to never let him go and to whisper the same love and endearment she deeply felt for him, but it was not right; she could not use his weakness to turn him around to desert Julie and take her instead. Set him free, and if he truly wanted her, he would come back and never leave again. But for now, he was betrothed to another woman, and that was the hard reality! Why did he never discuss Julie with her? She could not pry about his life, but he lived with Julie. How could he confess his concern for her? It's too confusing!

"Good night, Zach. Drive carefully. I'll see you tomorrow at the office bright and early." She waved to him as he drove away. She closed the door and leaned on the hard wood to shake off the coldness that suddenly gripped her. Why did Zach, all of a sudden, have seemingly a change of heart? Was there trouble in paradise between him and Julie, or had his conscience finally come to the harsh reality of where his true love lay? Lately, she observed him very attentively and was watchful of how he reacted to her requests. He had been calling her at odd times during weekends, with lame excuses, and on nights when Julie was away working part-time in the hospital. She knew something was not right. What was happening lately between her and Zach was getting to her nerves.

"Hello, Suzy, what's up? Glad you called- I really need someone to talk to these days. How was your trip?" With heaviness, Jasmine said exasperatingly, happy to unload her troubles upon a nice friend.

"Yeah, I was gone for a while; the trip went well. No trouble at all, same here, we all need someone once in a while, we can't let anything come between our friendship. I'm here to help, girl! I want to have a nice dinner with you! When are you not too busy?" Suzy wanted Jasmine to understand the relationship between Zach and Julie, having talked to them about their story. She had always been helpful to Jasmine with her advice. "How are you acting up to Zach's renewed amorous inkling? I thought you have grown accustomed to it and did not stir you up in any way?"

"I know that he cares a lot, but I'm still perplexed, and lately, I'm bothered with the way he's acting up about me. He, actually, just left. He came here bearing gifts, meaning Chinese food, my favorite, and confronted me with my feelings for him and, in so many ways, about his own feelings. But he was concerned and quite bothered with the latest news about my dinner date with Luke, a Navy guy, a younger brother of Sofia. She and her husband celebrated their first wedding anniversary and took Luke and me with them." Jasmine was a little edgy gathering her thoughts about what transpired between her and Zach, confused by her own emotions. "Zach wanted to know if Luke was my love interest and date. We were seen together by one of our officemates, Chelsea, who happened to be there. And guess what? Zach was also there, dining out with Julie at the same place, and I saw them just right across from our table. The lights were dim, and Zach was preoccupied with Julie and did not even notice I was there watching them. Take note, Julie was breathtakingly beautiful and very young, at the most, maybe about eighteen or so?"

"Really? What was the reason he came running to you? Are you aware of other reasons why Zach was fast-changing in his attitude toward you, and had he talked about Julie?" Suzy wanted to be clear of the circumstances before she could ask more questions, careful not to give Jasmine any idea that she knew more than she was letting on.

"No, nothing about Julie, except about needing more time for himself before making a decision- but he did not specify what kind of a decision. I could not fathom why, all of a sudden, he wanted to confront the past both of us had, buried a long time ago," she said. "I am sure I have moved on and have forgiven him deserting me; that is why I accepted and continued working with him. Now, I'm in this predicament, more complications involving another soul, hard to resolve. It's stronger, quite unrelenting, and too confusing for me to get to its roots without letting it surface completely in the open before I can even contemplate what and how to deal with it. It's somewhat complex and vague!"

"Sleep on it. Don't let your emotion go offhand and take it with a grain of salt; the situation will resolve, eventually. Cool heads always prevail! I'll pick you up tomorrow for dinner, hoping Zach will not call for another impromptu visit. This situation thrown on your path will get resolved, and we'll all laugh about it later, that I'm here to hold your hand and guide you through. See you then, good night." Both hung up.

"Good morning, Zach. How are you? I have here the reports you requested for the Montclaire account, and they look impressive. I'm sure the boss will be pleased with the figures." Jasmine laid the folder on his desk without looking at Zach directly. She wanted to display an air of disregard about the confrontation of the previous night. She moved gracefully to his outgoing box, picked up a bunch of papers, and looked through each while talking to him, "Anything you need that I can help you with?"

Zach moved away from his chair and circled his desk to reach out to Jasmine, "Don't tell me that what we talked about last night did not get through that pretty head of yours?" And while holding her hand with a caressing pressure, looked directly into her wide brown-eyed gaze, glimmering not with joy but with a dejected gleam, showing a sullen state of mind. He felt her silence but could not grasp what was still holding her back. He was as helpless as she was- with uncertainty looming over their relationship, he could not fathom how to explain his position and commitment to Julie without offending Jasmine's sentiments. She never mentioned nor asked about her. That was why he never opened up about his true relationship with her. He released her arm.

"Zach, we're both in a nightmare, probably not the worst yet, but let's take a deep breath and try our best to carry on. I'm sure the light of day will come to clear our foggy minds, and we'll resolve all issues, maybe in the most comfortable and convenient way. Yes, I'm deeply disturbed, and there is so much to do to find our peace, and I'll work that out with you. I'm in no position to ask or get involved in your way of life. I'll wait until the right time comes, but for now, let's just be as cordial and affable as we could possibly be to avoid stress and tension. Okay?" After locking eyes with him, she nodded and gave him a glum smile, and out the door, she went without looking back.

Zach was left alone digesting every word spoken by Jasmine, trying to decipher her state of mind relative to the truth of the affair confronting them. He knew his position was graver than Jasmine's because of Julie, his responsibility. He was lost in his thoughts, wondering how to resolve the issue at hand without emotionally injuring anyone concerned-least of all Julie, who was not at fault here. He knew Julie had no one except him. Would Jasmine understand his choice, his promises, and the responsibility he took on for Julie and her life?

Jasmine met Suzy a few blocks away from her office to have dinner and continue their talk about the previous night. Jasmine detailed her conversation and how it affected both Zach and her. "I'm confused more than ever. I've come to the conclusion that I'm not really over him since the pain is still here, but I'm just ignoring it, trying to bury it to be able to go on with life." She tried to subdue the tears that wanted to wet her eyes. "And the reality is harsher than what I believe. I never could open up to tell him about how much his relationship with Julie was bothering me."

"I know it will be harder because you're acting, trying to downplay your emotions, but you're not totally in control. You're more overwhelmed than you think." Suzy felt compassion seeing her in distress like this. "Okay, this is not a pep talk, but you're not at fault; there is no blame game here. Neither of the three of you should feel guilty, least of all Julie. She eventually will bear the worst loss, unless Zach is pressured into living with her, or makes him feel guilty for not having anyone to help her, which makes him accept responsibility until she can care for herself."

"What do you mean, until she would be able to be on her own taking care of herself? What about their getting married in the near future?"

"Before I left that night to fly to San Francisco, I went to see Zach with Joven and a friend, Charlie; you don't know him. They took me to Zach's place for a barbecue, and I was able to meet Julie, who lives with Zach, which we both know about. What we didn't know was his true connection or relation to Julie." Suzy stopped talking to make sure Jasmine fully understood every word she was saying.

"What is known about them is that they are engaged and would, of course, eventually get married unless I talked him out of it and asked him to marry me instead." Jasmine intercepted with an obvious grim in her voice.

"You don't need to be sarcastic and don't need to beat yourself hard, silly." She looked at Jasmine on how she would react to the next few words she was to drop on her, which would either shatter her world into pieces or make her the happiest she had ever been for quite a long time now. "Zach and Julie are not lovers, not engaged to be married, now or in the future!"

"What? Don't play havoc with my emotions or toy with my heart; that's not fair!" Her brown eyes, wide open with mixed emotions, were imploring Suzy.

"Zach, actually, consented to Charlie's idea to invite me to explain to you his circumstances in life- the many things he had no courage to open up and discuss with you without stirring painful memories from your past life with him. He told me, he promised his best friend who passed away from a malignant brain tumor, that he would take care of his baby sister Julie until she could finish her college degree and could be on her own. He never took the time to correct the wrong rumors about his relationship, about Julie living with him."

"How come he did not tell me anything about it even when Chelsea openly told us she had seen them together that same night? I was there witnessing it myself."

"He never wanted to talk about Julie- it was better that way, instead of being defensive. And he was hiding it from you because he knew you would not understand, especially with the problem the two of you were having- of your long estrangement. He knew you would never conform to his decision of taking care of Julie personally and for a long while more!"

"I think I'm the one at fault for not being lenient with him in many ways. I was very possessive and selfish, and that's why he thought I could not handle his problem with Julie. Loving him the way I did, in spite of his lack of attention when we were in school, made him doubtful about me. And the reason he came forward now was because of his concern for seeing me depressed and antisocial, knowing I cared for him before and thinking I'm still head over heels in love with him. And having Julie as his sole responsibility made it complicated."

"Whatever, love has played the three of you, and there is no fault in loving back; it comes when you least expect it, plays havoc, or showers joy to the lucky ones. Zach was doubtful how his potent love for you could materialize when Julie came into the picture, at a time when he wanted you back in his life but was unsure how you would accept Julie in his life. Zach could find happiness, and even Julie would not have a hold on his heart when he would decide to walk his way back to your heart eventually. Julie would just be a temporary thing in your lives."

"It's hard to ignore him because we always talk and work together, at the office or at home, when he calls in need of some information about clients. I am the one who should take hold of myself and not mistake his gestures as love or desire. But it's harder to play cool and unaffected by his nearness; maybe I should just resign and go elsewhere to find another job. Or get a boyfriend to avoid Zach altogether." Jasmine was looking directly at the comforting glimmer of hope in Suzy's kind eyes.

"Zach will be furious at me, but I can introduce you to my brother's friend. He's handsome and tall, your type, yeah, that's what I told my brother when I first saw Liam Simons with him at a family gathering at home when I was just 12 years old. He was with us a few weeks ago- too bad you were on vacation at that time. I even kidded him about you, and he said not to forget to invite him again and that he will look forward to meeting you. Heck, that's what I'll do on my birthday next week, just a few of us at home. I'll call Liam and then invite Zach to bring Julie with him, so the two of you can check each other out. We need to have everything in the open, no more secrets."

When Jasmine was back at the office, she tried to bury herself in her work and saw Zach again, a few more times before she was glad to call it a day. She skipped her usual 'goodbye, have a nice day, see you tomorrow' speech and hurriedly went directly to the elevator but was surprised to see Zach waiting for her. "I'll walk you to your car. Don't say no, and just keep on walking with that beautiful smile on your face for everyone to see who crosses our way."

And she did just what Zach asked for and was finally glad to say what was at the tip of her tongue- away from any eavesdropper. "Zach, please stop torturing me. I'm truly unprepared for this bombshell you have unwittingly dropped on me. Don't resurrect the ghost of the past; it's not funny."

"No, I can't. I have no choice but to confront reality. We have a say on this and what will happen to us. I will not blindly take steps anymore without making sure it's the right one for both of us, regardless of any complication, situation, or discomfort we may encounter along the way."

"And how do you plan to do that? Torture me with inquisitiveness and demand answers that will soothe your oversolicitous ego and further bruise mine?" She shook her head to indicate her negative attitude and her determination to let the past lie dormant for eternity- deny themselves the happiness they had wished for, too elusive to hold due to their circumstances.

"Are you afraid of the truth?" He asked and put his hand against the car door as she was trying to open it, searching her eyes for the truth, looking very appealing and commanding in his ways, sending warmth to Jasmine's heart.

"No, I'm not afraid of the truth. In fact, let me recite it back to you- Yes, Zach, when I was much younger and foolish, I thought you were in love with me, and I with you, but later, when you left without a word, I was crushed and realized the greatest folly of **_unrequited love_**. Thereafter, I crawled back, rose up, shook the dust off myself, and vowed to come out of my foolish dreams and be real in my pathetic life for once. There you have it, let me go, please?" Zach pulled away from her, more stunned than before, more confused and for the first time, felt a strong squeeze in his gut. Bewildered, he stayed on the side until her car was gone from view before he started walking toward his car.

Zach lay in bed awake, thinking of what Jasmine said verbatim. That was the hard, cold truth, and he just realized the cruelty he caused Jasmine all the six years without communication between them. He knew he did not, once or ever, tell her he loved her, but his actions spoke louder than words; they were unspoken but obvious and were accepted by everyone, except by himself most probably, egotistically. Nonetheless, his love had seared and scorched its way to Jasmine's subconscious and made her the way she was then and now. Still, the stronghold of love lived in them!

Feeling ill, forsaken one more time, Jasmine staggered to maintain her sanity and wondered if she could sustain herself for another day with the complexity of the situation and the foreboding sense of vulnerability in Zach's presence. After her admission of her unrequited love for Zach, she felt she bared her soul to him, leaving her defenseless and subject to abject speculation and ridicule from him.

Zach was at her office when she walked in, "Good morning, Zach. What do you need or are in search of this early?" She put her jacket on the rack and her handbag inside the drawer without even casting a side glance at Zach, who was meticulously looking at her. She was always impeccably dressed, classy and appealing, showing her long, beautifully shaped legs, one of her strong assets. He was always in awe, contemplating her beauty.

"I saw you out of the elevator, so I thought to just wait here and pick up the readout from yesterday so you don't have to come to my office. I'm saving you legwork! That's the reason why I'm here, no hidden agenda or what you always refer to as bull."

"Just the same, it's hard to really know what you're up to, seriously. But, give me a few minutes, and I'll get them out from my files. Have a seat; it won't take long." She sat opposite him and clicked away from her computer, located the file, and set her printer to spit out the requested figures. Very effectively, as he would say.

"Is there anything else I can do for you?" He looked at her trying to convey his feelings, but Jasmine gave him a smile that was hard to figure out. She was getting better with her game of denying him access to her vulnerable achy heart. He took his eyes off her and studied the figures, seated there for a while, intentionally longer than necessary, until he could make Jasmine a little uncomfortable. He then stood right there in front of her desk, tapped his fingers, and said, "See me in my office with the files of Alaska, Inc. before coffee break, will you?"

She stood up, looked at him, and nodded, "Is that all?"

"Have coffee with me in my office instead of going to the cafeteria, okay?" He gave her a very provocative smile, like he was sure of himself, sure that he'll win this game.

Soon as Zach left her desk, the phone rang, and Suzy said, "Hello, beautiful, did you sleep well? Can you come? I talked to my bro and asked him to bring Liam Simons to dinner tomorrow. I can't wait until my birthday- I want you guys to make the acquaintance so that you're both comfortable with each other by the time we have the party."

"Okay, what time do you want me to come? Shall I bring food?" She was eager to make it to her place tomorrow and meet Liam Simons, the handsome friend and an associate of Jasper, Suzy's brother.

"No, silly, we'll make it like an impromptu meeting. You'll come by from work to drop off a book that I've been asking you to lend me, and then I'll invite you to stay for dinner since my brother will be visiting with a friend. Okay?"

"Sure, hey, thanks, at least I've something to think about instead of my rotten problems. See you then, bye." She hung up, happy to know that at least she would be meeting a guy whom she would not be worried about if he was as weird as others who tried to pick her up at the mall or at the beach. She was picky with men seeking friendship, afraid of those who preyed on vulnerable women. She hoped Liam Simons was as handsome and tall as the Navy guy. She did not like to get involved with men in the military, fear of losing a loved one in battle, that situation she could not even dare to think.

It was 9:30 am, and she was just about to leave her desk when her intercom rang. It was Zach reminding her to bring the file of Alaska, Inc. and get some figures for the new subsidiary. It was a legitimate business inquiry, not just an excuse to get her to his office. It, nevertheless, made her wary of discomfort in the event Zach would bring up the same topic from last time's encounter. She was afraid of many things about herself, her own feelings and vulnerability, Zach's state of mind, his sensitiveness, and his relationship and responsibility with Julie. And now, about this new guy who would be involved with her somehow in the future. She hoped he would help calm the overheating situation between her and her boss and give her a sense of closure to once and for all resolve the prevailing predicament with Zach.

She knocked twice, noticed the sign 'Do not disturb' hanging on the door, and tried to open the door, but Zach was right there opening the door for her and then turned the knob to lock the door. "Here, please be seated." He took the files from her and placed them on top of his desk. He took the paper where the figures were printed and right away input them into the file he was working on. For a while, he looked at the file and hit send on the email he had just composed. He set aside other things on the desk, called the operator, and said, "Betty, hold my calls and Jasmine's too. She's here with me; please take messages. Okay?" He stood up and asked Jasmine to follow him to the corner of the office, where a counter was set up for coffee or drinks served to clients. He pointed to a nice chair for her to sit while he poured coffee for them. Jasmine was quiet but apprehensive about what kind of conversation the two of them would be engaged in. At this point, she knew it was no longer an official business matter that they would be talking about. *"Maybe another monkey business or could be about Julie,"* Jasmine thought.

"How are you, Jazz? I was not able to sleep thinking of the impropriety I made against our friendship, the sharp edge of the truth between us in the past. I have been meaning to talk to you about this- ask for forgiveness, for putting you through what you have been through. I'm sorry for not acknowledging you, your presence, and your kindness in my life before. I treated you unkindly by evading and not acknowledging the raw truth of my desertion. Every time I thought about it, the more I lost the courage to confront my own deficiency and lack of integrity." He showed compassion and was really in pain dealing with his past actions.

"Zach, I would be lying if I told you that I did not suffer during the long years of your silence, but I don't blame you for your mistake; your actions came from being young and being irresponsible, for not confronting your demons. How many of us in our younger days were not guilty of that? Do not punish yourself for the poor decisions your youth made. The important thing is realizing what you did was wrong and owning the accountability for those mistakes. But the past is past, and it could never be undone; we can not go back and do it over, the way we think now is how it should have been done."

She looked Zach in the eye and really meant what she was saying. "Let's move on, bury the past behind us. We have learned the lessons that would guide us to prevent ourselves from repeating history again. I know how you care, and you worry a lot about me, don't be. I'm a big girl now, and I can take care of myself. I'm taking my time; I'm not in a hurry, but I know I will find love again. We were not meant to be; that is why things happened the way they did. I realize that now, and I want you to accept that, too. You have a responsibility to handle Julie, and I think it is great you're helping her, don't change anything on my account."

He sat before her, and he hugged her tight, "God knows how much I care for you, and I want you to be happy. I thought I could talk, show you my love, but you're refusing to accept me back in your heart." He stared outside the window, trying to compose himself, before he continued,

"Julie is not my lover. I temporarily adopted her until she's stable enough to be on her own, living together while putting our lives in perspective. We support each other, helping each other mend our broken lives. When I realized I needed you in my life, I was too far gone and was afraid of rejection and did not know where to find you."

"You came looking for me?" She was surprised to learn that from him but was happy to at least he was sorry for leaving her.

"I did. In fact, I wrote to your address, but my letter was returned- that was how I lost hope and became despondent for not doing the right thing. When I finally came back to California, I looked for your name but did not find anything, until I asked one of my friends who knew people who would be glad to work in our company, because I was desperate for good workers. Your name was on the list he gave me; that was how I tracked you down via a headhunter and offered you this job."

She now knew how Zach found her. And she was so happy having him back in her life until she found out about Julie, their relationship, and her living with him. She went to work for him but kept her distance because of Julie. She did not show any interest in Zach because she was respecting his relationship with the woman of his choice, and that was when she had totally lost hope of ever winning him again. Zach treated her with respect and was very professional in his dealings with her, and never did dwell about their past together- just an apology but no detailed explanation. It was sort of a taboo. That was how their relationship was until recently, when all hell broke loose.

The fact that Zach confessed his circumstances with Julie as something solid and the convenience of living together made her more confused and uncertain. Here, she was seated in front of him, telling her the whole truth from when he started looking for her and up to when he came to her house, confronting her of their past, which she had thought had been buried a long time ago. Now in full view, resurrected before her, stunned, perplexed, and confused, she could not cope with the bare truth before her. Could she ever trust him? Why was he able to play his part, so well, distant and respectful, for over a year now without telling her anything? Did he ever crave for her company, her nearness? Where was love that grew fonder because of absence? The tears she was trying to hold came rushing out of her eyes like a dam breached, bursting with water, the flood of her pent-up emotions.

Only in her dreams! Only in fiction stories, in movies to have a complex and exciting plot and intrigue! She wiped her tears and straightened up, and got ready to leave when Zach stood up, pulled her to him and embraced her tightly, and again whispered, "I'm so sorry if you're overwhelmed by the past, give it a while, and everything will clear up." He put his finger and lifted her chin, looked her in the eyes, and said once more, "I knew this would be hard on you, but I've waited long enough; it's time to let the cat out of the bag. Don't worry about Julie- she has grown dear to me as a little sister, and as soon as she's finished her schooling and gets a job, she'll be on her own. We'll be left to sort our lives."

Would she? What if they fell in love with each other, being close and at times amorous as what she had seen at the restaurant that night? Was she jealous of Julie because she was young and breathtakingly beautiful? Zach was a virile man who had needs and desires! Will Zach turn his attention to Julie if she gives him a hard time? She knew he always went the extra mile for people he cared about, stepping up to the plate to do good, if not the best. His word was always as dependable as tomorrow's rising of the sun. It did not take much to warm Jasmine's blood- his kindness entitled him to a bit more leeway than the rest of mankind. He was one of a kind; that was why she loved him with a passion that never paled in comparison to the real thing yet had lain dormant for a long time, now surfacing more intensely each time she laid eyes on him.

"Zach, I have no right over you. Remember, you never told me you loved me or gave me any reason to think that way. There is no need to make a mountain out of a molehill- you made no promises, there was no tie that bound you." She looked away as she spoke the truth. They were both slaves of their own desires, unspoken.

Zach was stunned to look back, but there were several moments in time when his desires would burn up, but he knew better than to start something he could not finish. He was, once more, in that same predicament- he wanted her but could not take her. Their eyes locked, and both knew the sudden, intense awareness that settled in a ball the size of an iceberg striking down their guts. Jasmine stood up and walked to the door, and Zach was too helpless to hold her back and would wait for another time to settle their differences.

Part #2

Jasmine started to dress up to go to Suzy's place to meet Jasper and his friend. She was nervous about their plan, but she had promised to show up. There was no harm in joining them even if she was not interested in Jasper's friend. It turned out to be a good get-together with Suzy, and Jasper was always happy to connect with friends.

"Hello, Jasmine, I haven't seen you since you left Suzy's company. How have you been?" Jasper asked, extending his hand to Jasmine and ushering her inside.

"Hi, Jasper, it's nice to see you again. How's San Francisco? Suzy just visited you there a few weeks ago. What brought you here so soon?" Jasmine adorning a smile, followed Jasper inside and looked around.

"Where's Suzy?"

"Come, they are in the backyard, we're barbecuing some ribs, and I have a friend who came with me. Let me introduce him to you."

"Sue, Jasmine is here." He said to his sister and signaled his friend to come by the table. "Jasmine, this is Liam, a friend and associate. Liam, meet Jasmine, Sue's former officemate."

Liam approached her and, with his dark blue-gray eyes, contemplated the beauty that stood in front of him, "I'm very pleased to meet you. I'm Liam Simons, a long-time friend of the family." He extended his hand for a handshake.

"Hi, Jasmine Warloffe." She mused as she shook his hands, "Suzy and I have been friends since I started working with her, but sadly, I left the company in search of a greener pasture." She uttered a soft laugh at her own joke.

Jasmine was pleased to meet Liam, a tall guy with mesmerizing blue-gray eyes, very intense and expressive. It felt as if he was searching for her soul when he looked at her. He was not movie-actor handsome, but he had a kind of rugged masculinity and raw appeal, topped with a sexy, intriguing look that could send one to the roof. He was quite attractive, and she innocently wondered how many lips might have been crushed by his kisses. Maybe, someday, she won't mind her lips being crushed too, perhaps!

"Well, well, there you are, my dear. Did you smell the barbecue from where you live?" Suzy said, with a knowing wink, to her friend.

"Nope, a loan on a book, and whoa! Lucky me to get to taste some of that good smelling barbecue you guys are cooking and for meeting one of Jasper's good friends, Liam, here." Jasmine was surely glad this was a very fortunate meeting because she was happy to have met Liam, quite a guy. Still, an eligible bachelor. She hoped that none had yet pinned the heartthrob down.

"How could Suzy not, in the least, be interested in such an attractive gentleman?" She said to herself.

Liam commented on Jasmine's remark about changing jobs, "Don't we all seek greener pastures? That's the way to climb the corporate ladder these days, hop from one employer to another until you get the best. I did that for a while, too, until I formed my own company."

"Oh, if you don't mind my asking, what kind of business interest does your company deal with?" Jasmine asked.

"I'm an Architect, just like my friend here, Jasper, an Engineer who is in the construction business. We go together like a horse and carriage." He looked at Jasper, laughing, and gave him a friendly punch on the shoulder.

"Isn't that said about marriage? You have a sense of humor. For a while there, I stopped to contemplate. Yeah, you're right. You draw, he builds!" Jasmine was beaming at his ingenious quip.

"You got it! You can't have one without the other!" They all laughed about it and kept the humor coming for a lively afternoon. By the time they were finished, they seemed to have reached a good friendly bonding. Liam and Jasmine promised to be in touch exchanging numbers and a repeat of the camaraderie.

That evening, Jasmine was feeling a bit offbeat, reminiscing about her encounter with Liam, who was a very personable guy. She turned on the music, and instantly her mind followed the beat. Her mood switched to a better place and left Zach behind for a while. She was constantly pondering on Liam's looks, warmth, and friendliness.

Zach and Liam were both tall and handsome, with raw sex appeal, but in personality, they immensely differed. Liam was funny, direct, warm with no reservation, friendly, and simply sweet. While Zach was more reserved, a little conservative, commanding, but nice and kind-hearted. They were both worthy of love and affection from any lucky woman they chose to love.

She was a person who could tell right away if a man was her type as she could instantly feel the chemistry and attraction, though not all handsome guys had that effect on her. She was of age, but her experience with love was limited to her young devotion to Zach in high school, unrequited! When meeting someone, she knew right away whether she would learn to care in the long run. Would her heart beat for the right reason this time? Would it be different or the same with Liam? She wasn't sure, but she wanted to know him better. Could there be a possibility they would get closer? She never had any interest in any of the men she had met before, but Liam had sparked something within her. She fell asleep with that in her subconscious.

And when she awoke the following morning, she felt as if it was a new day, a new beginning with new hope. She could leave behind all the heartaches of yesteryears and focus on the coming life. There's a lot to look forward to. Perhaps Liam, her new friend, could make her days lighter and worth living, and eventually, Zach, with time, would disappear from her subconscious.

The Sunday weekend was sunnier and warmer. She felt like doing some gardening and spending time in her backyard, which had been neglected for a while. Good that her neighbor's son was very industrious. He always kept her lawn well mowed.

Dressed in her comfortable shorts and a loose shirt, ready to work outside, she opened her freezer, took a chunk of pork butt meat, a packet of burrito mix, and a can of refried beans from her pantry, together with a good-sized green pepper and a few stalks of celery, sliced, she threw everything in a big slow cooker at high heat, before picking up her gardening tools and proceeded to tackle her chores in the garden.

Her stargazer lilies were starting to bloom, emitting their fragrance, while her climbing clematis of different varieties was already in full bloom, lending a mixed color galore along her trellises. Her peonies were competing with her climbing roses of yellow, pink, and white blooms. The atmosphere emitted with the sweet smell of roses, and Jasmine sat peacefully in the tranquil serenity of her sweet-smelling garden.

This was why she never got tired of doing her gardening stuff, no matter how busy her work life was. It took away the loneliness. Each time she appreciated the beauty and smelt the scent of her blooms. The shade of a big flowering tree never got tired of providing the coolness that was needed when the midday sun was at its hottest peak. At the same time, the shade provided her the privacy she craved for.

She was in deep meditation, enjoying her surroundings, when her phone rang, and she saw that it was Zach. "Hello Zach, did I miss anything at work?" She tried to remember if she had to submit a rush job in the computer room or not.

"Nothing that I know of, actually, I am right here at the office. I came in for a few things that needed some updating. I'm starving, so I thought of you, in case you would like to have lunch with me...." He left his sentence hanging a bit like a subtle request.

"Oh, sorry, I can't, to tell you the truth, I have started a big job here. I was doing a bit of gardening and made some burritos in my slow cooker, ready for lunch by now. If you care for Mexican food, you can come over and join me. We can eat burritos in my garden."

"Nothing could be better than that, love it, be there in 15 minutes or so. Do you want me to pick up anything? Beer, drinks, or fruits?" He sounded delighted at the invitation of lunch at her place. The invite made Zach feel warmer and happy, knowing that Jasmine was finally coming out to accept his presence in her life once again.

"Anything but flowers! I'm in the middle of a lot of blooms, so you don't have to bring me flowers." Her mind clicked a memory of the song 'You Don't Bring me Flowers Anymore,' A duet sung by Streisand and Neil Diamond. But she hoped that Zach would not lose interest in her, as did the lover in the song.

He rang the bell, and Jasmine promptly opened the gate to let his car into the driveway, then closed the gate and ushered him to the backyard. He brought some beer, soft drinks, and ice cream. She had already set up a round table near her tool shed with a cooler nearby.

The moment Zach entered her garden, he could smell the appetizing slow-cooked meat sitting in the middle of the table. The tortillas were kept in a container for warmth, and she had also placed some plates and plenty of napkins for the coming mess of her sumptuous pregnant burritos. He had eaten burritos before in Mexican restaurants, but her home prepared ones were better, with very tender pork almost pulled to perfection with the tasty saucy beans and soft veggies over a warm tortilla. He wanted to eat more than he could, but his appreciation of the moment was more gratifying to him than anything else.

Jasmine sharing her lunch and precious time with him in a beautiful setting amidst her scented flowers made it doubly satisfying. It had been a while since she had treated him so nicely.

"What are you thinking about, work?" She asked, smiling sweetly at him, trying to guess the thing that preoccupied his mind at this lovely moment.

"Far from that, here, the way we are, happy, tranquil, and just enjoying the moment, with the soft, easy music of your player. It's just truly amazing. How many times I have not thought of slowing down, to relax, and just going with the flow of life."

"I love music. I can't live without it. I try to feel the emotions, especially in sad country songs. The depiction of heartaches often brings tears to my eyes."

Zach just realized from the conversation what made Jasmine's heart cold and her prevailing attitude hardened. It all came from her preoccupation, always reliving her own heartaches when listening to sad songs. The sad lyrics were doubling, if not multiplying, the intensity of her loss.

"Wouldn't you agree that getting too serious in analyzing the words of the sad songs drives your subconscious toward the emotions that once made you sad? And then it stays with you, and you lose control of how you see things. Sad thoughts evoke sadness, whereas happy thoughts bring happiness." He studied her body language for some sign, whether his words were making some sense to her.

"I know, but I'm helpless and alone, and at times I have nothing to do but brood on what might have been. The question of where did I go wrong is always hanging over my head." She desperately confessed and looked through those eyes where the blueness always warmed her soul.

"Jazz, you did no wrong. You and I were players, and, at our early age, we did not have the wise concept of the sages. We were untamed and foolish. Willing to grab whatever came toward us. Since it did not turn out well, we could not turn back the hands of time. All we have to do is take it with a grain of salt, strive harder, and vow to change our fate hereinafter. Would you be willing to try? For us?"

"What are you asking me to do, Zach?" She asked. Her eyes, shaded with uncertainty and full of doubts, looked into his soul.

"I'm not asking you to undo the past. All I'm asking is for us to be happy. We found each other again! We have lost the time that can never be recovered, but we can move on, leave behind the sad, undesirable hurt, and make the best of what is left in us. That is what I'm asking you to try with me."

Jasmine remained silent after searching for the truth from his soulful eyes. Would she try, would she give themselves a chance, at least, to recapture the attraction they had for one another? What about Julie? Would her presence in Zach's life hinder their willingness to coordinate their lives together? The desire to try was not good enough. She had to have firm faith and trust in order for it to work, but she knew, at times, love was not enough!

Zach pulled his chair closer to her, took her hand in his, and then tilted her chin with his finger. He looked her in those big beautiful brown eyes, searching for the much-awaited answer that could open the door and make life easier for both of them.

Jasmine closed her eyes as she could not bear the intensity of his emotions. She only opened them up when Zach's smooth fingers started caressing her lips. The emotion she felt was being drawn in, like the proverbial moth attracted to candlelight by the warmth of his fingertips. She was in a trance-like state when Zach's lips brushed hers lightly, like a feather touch, but the impact was likened to a bombshell force!

In the past, Zach was never bold. He had brushed his lips, always lightly on her cheeks or on her head, but never on her lips. When she did not protest, he locked eyes with her and deepened the kiss, slow but with passion. His lips lingered near hers in a long, loving, and meaningful kiss. Their first in a decade of knowing each other.

"I'm not going to apologize for that. It's been a long time coming." He said, still holding her hand, caressing it with thumb pressure on her palm.

"Please, Jazz, open your heart, let me in. I want to be back in your life. We both suffered much already. I can't live knowing your heart is as hardened as a cold stone because of the past. Give me a chance to love you, and I'll do my best to make up for the long lonely years between us."

She tried to avoid looking at him; instead, her fingers toyed with her glass. She was quiet for a while, then she sat up with her back against her chair and said, "All right, Zach, you win. We'll try your way, but please go slow. My heart is so fragile. I, myself, am not in total control."

He was overjoyed to hear her say what he had wanted to hear for a long time. He went ahead, took her lips again, and kissed her, this time with passion.

He looked at her and said, "Jazz, please open your mouth for me the way you opened your heart. I want to taste your sweetness." As Jazz opened her mouth, Zach's tongue went inside and touched hers and tasted her for the first time. The sweetness of their first passionate real kiss made him feel as if he was in heaven with her.

Jasmine's eyes glimmered with joy like a pool of melted chocolate, drawing him to her gaze and Zach's tongue went deeper into her mouth. He seemed to enjoy the ecstasy and wanted to stay there forever, arousing deep and raw sensuality. As she returned the gaze into his blue eyes like the deep blue sea, it was easy to drown her loneliness and tomorrow's worries. Her womanly scent was mouth-watering, whetting his senses with a fierce desire to possess her. With the urgent mating instinct throbbing between his legs, the elemental force between the sexes made him crazy. It drove his passion to a fever pitch.

But his better judgment won over his little head's desire to go overboard. He did not want to scare her and must abide by her request to go slow. It was the hardest thing to do, to cool down his guard and let go of passion for the meantime.

Just as it did to Jasmine, he was glad that he was in a better position to make the call. They both held hands and talked while enjoying the rest of the afternoon in the breezy coolness of the shade underneath the spread of the tree. Before he left, he went inside the house with Jasmine for more casual storytelling, and when he was about to leave, Zach, once more, was enslaved by his hot desire to take Jasmine into an intimate embrace both stood lost in the heat of their wanton desire for each other.

"I want you so badly. One of these days, I'll lose control and take you completely with me all the way, but for now, I'll give us a reprieve, for tomorrow never ends. There'll be a propitious time for us to catch up and enjoy serene intimacy to our heart's delight. Wouldn't that be nice, my love?"

And in between his sweet talk, he was ravishing her lips, crushing, almost bruising them, but there was a fine line between pain and the joy of ecstasy! Jasmine wanted to tell him to stay and be lost in paradise with him while the world stood still. They had waited for this moment to come, to happen between them. Who cares about propriety? They were two consenting adults, and there was no complexity between them, except for a business named Julie! That thought threw cold water on her whetting appetite for Zach's lovemaking. And she let go!

"I'll see you tomorrow, bright and early. Thank you, Zach. Good day, drive safely." She said and followed him to his car. They kissed each other again, this time lighter but sweet. She opened the gate by her remote and waved goodbye as the car disappeared from her view.

Her days were really improving to her heart's content in just a matter of weeks. Her reconciliation with Zach was foremost, and then there was the enjoyable meeting with Liam. She was in a contemplative mood when the phone rang, and Liam's number popped up.

"Well, look who's calling, Liam!" She was happy to receive his first call to her.

"Hello, there, how are you? Thank you for remembering who I am! That was nice instead of 'Liam, who? Have you had your dinner?'" He asked like it was his concern to fatten herself.

"Yes, I normally have dinner by 7 in the evening, that way, if I stay late, I can have a light snack of milk and Oreo." She said with a little chuckle. She found it easy to have witty remarks with Liam. He had the wholesome, funny way of his own interpretation of things.

"Oreo? That's not a healthy choice. I had the impression that you're one of those who are hung up on baking their own cookies." He joked in an attempt to perk up her mood.

"Rich coming from you! Do you watch your diet? You must be quite health-conscious as you have a lean but strong frame, no flabby abs!" She described his attractive masculine figure, trying to picture him in her mind.

"That's a plus. You even remembered my lean but sturdy frame! That's very impressive and quite encouraging. Thank you for remembering my name and my looks. Now I know you're not just guessing who you're really talking to!"

"I'm truthful. I speak my mind. I like you, that's why I remembered. Had you been one of those nondescript persons, I would not even take your call. I really enjoyed meeting and interacting with you, and now I understand why you and Jasper are friends. I know Jasper as a very respectable guy, and he won't be friends with people of questionable characters. That's how confident I am with you. I'm at ease like I've known you long enough to kid around you."

"Wow, that's something, thank you! I hope I can live up to your expectations. I like you more. You typify a very practical and smart lady. Just like you said, we have a commonality. We're friends with people like Jasper and Suzy." He said, counting on their concept of the kind of people they both wanted to be friends with.

"You will. I'm not hard to please. I'm easy and open. I don't hide behind a complex façade. I find that honesty makes one very acceptable and commands more respect and transparency. I don't go around the bush or tiptoe my way to avoid giving my take or verdict on certain things." She openly laid before him what she was and what she expected from him in return.

"You have my vote right away. That's the way I want an acquaintance to be. To know and grow with and find more grounds to explore towards a lasting, more meaningful friendship. Not be afraid to ask and find out what they stand for. I salute your courage to stand for what you believe in." Liam was open about what he wanted in a friend, and they seemed to have a consensus on the matter.

"If it's not too early to ask, I'd like to know if you have someone you could call a very special person who enjoys a lot of privileges?" He listened very carefully and sensed her reluctance to answer his question with pointed precision.

"Did you mean a relationship as my fiance or just a person I have a crush on, or an ordinary boyfriend who sees me regularly, a suitor? You have to be specific to get the accurate answer." She said, wanting clarity on his inquiry.

"I'm sure if you're engaged, you could have said that to my face, so maybe that was not what I meant." He bounced back the ball wittingly to her court.

"Okay, then, you're right. If I was engaged, I would have been flaunting that with pride. Well, who does not have a knight in shining armor? Even at a very young age, I knew the wonderful traits of the man I would give my heart to. How he looks, how he treats women and family, etc." She tried to play it cool so as not to discuss Zach with him. Suzy could have mentioned her intriguing past.

"So, there's someone special that would be tough to compete with in winning your heart!" He deduced from her statement, which was what he had expected anyway. She was educated, smart, and working, with an attractive personality, but she had that evasive air about her personal privacy.

"You can say that, who at my age would not have personally pinned, or at least, daydreamed about a romance made in fantasy land? In a few years, I would've been tagged as a spinster." She said a bit in worry. Why couldn't she admit to the naked truth about her broken heart? Was it recently unbroken by a passionate kiss by Zach? She gave herself the chance to bounce the ball back to his court. "How about you? Do you have something I need to know about in matters of the heart?"

"Had I been laid or unlucky in love? Guess I won't be able to pass up the question. But as it is, yes, I have had relationships in my past, nothing lasting because of a lot of factors. At the present time, I'm dating, but nothing intriguing or exciting to tell."

"Aha, just passing by, watching and speculating, nothing special? Is that it?" Jasmine countered with the funny way she put it.

"Something like that! Why do you know? Do you have a brother or close male friend?" He mused curiously. Liam pondered on the matter and her secrets. He seemed interested in her and her little world. Was it life that offered her a chance to gain some knowledge?

He was very curious at how successfully she was fencing wittingly with him. "Tell me about this dream guy, the knight in shining armor. I want to know if I can compete with him."

"Nothing much to tell, except he's tall, educated, and handsome like you. My love, if you may call it, was unrequited. I have been a silent admirer since then. I care not to count it or label it as a fellow of love. So, there is nothing to tell except for my shattered ego and battered feelings. I was broken-hearted, and for a long time, I was wearing the gloom on my sleeves. He knew nothing about my adulation. He left town and was gone." She could not add the fact of his return until recently.

"You don't know where he is today?" Liam asked. That was the question she was trying to avoid, but there it was. How could she explain? She did not want to tell a lie or be evasive.

She said softly, as casually and nonchalantly as she could, "Oh, of course, people who left town to search for their places in the sun, some of them eventually came back. He did too."

"So, what happened to your unrequited love? Did he finally realize what a fool he was? Was your love finally acknowledged and returned?" He said in a rapid succession of questions, getting more excited and waiting in anticipation.

"I don't know yet, but he's here, backtracking his steps. I'll keep you posted if and when something finally happens. Alright? It's getting late, and tomorrow I have to work early."

"Okay, hey, don't feel bad, stay positive and remember I'm here for you. I'll talk to you soon. You take care and chin up. I'm rooting for you. Good night, bye." He hung up. Jasmine felt bad about not telling him about her newfound hope in Zach, looking back to their past. Not only did he offer a heartfelt apology, but he also promised to truly make amends.

As usual, Zach found Jasmine in the computer room, making sure she had no job that needed any rerun. "You're surely an early bird. Did you catch a lot of worms for our breakfast? Let's have some coffee. I want to run something by you."

"Let me just print the recap of Alaska, Inc. I know you'll need it right away." She said as she rushed to the printer.

Over a cup of coffee that Zach had poured for her, she was toying with an idea of how Zach would be acting when they were together at the office, like this time. She did not want anybody being alerted about their newfound understanding, especially Chelsea, whose reactions were instantaneous and uninhibited.

She did not want Zach to get embarrassed, whose circumstances with Julie had not been fully exploited. "Zach, about us, can we stay uncommitted and unaffected for the sake of others? I want to spare you any discomfort about Julie, I know it's nobody's business, but still, tongues would continue wagging, regardless."

At first, Zach was not sure about her request and the reason why she proposed such a thing, but sound or not, she had the right to judge what was more expedient for their situation. They were cold and distant before, and to see them in a reverse mode, lovey-dovey and inseparable now, would surely raise a lot of concern with people around them. "Sure, I understand the situation, and I'll leave it to you to decide on how we would take this in stride."

"What was that you wanted to run by me about?" She asked, remembering what he had said earlier.

"I wanted to invite you to dinner tonight, at home, with Julie, so that the two of you could finally meet. Would that be alright? Go home early, and I'll pick you up at 7 tonight."

"That would be fine." She could not think of any valid reason for rejecting the dinner offer with him and Julie. Having seen a glimpse of her, she was just perfect, young, and breathtakingly beautiful. Was she now afraid of competition? Were those the same reasons that held Zach's heart captive, not wanting to let go of her? When these thoughts invaded her mind, was she jealous of Julie? Finally, discarding the thoughts, she conceded, "I'll be ready by seven."

Coffee with Zach in the early hours of the morning was fine before they retrieved their report recaps from the computer room because there were no people observing their every move. The whole day went by smoothly, with a few intercom phone calls with Zach, but there were no endearing words exchanged. Afraid of some eavesdroppers. At about 5 pm, she knocked on Zach's office to let him know she was on her way home.

When Zach came by to pick her up, he alighted from his car to catch her before she closed the door. He took her hand and ushered her back inside the house, and there he beheld her sweetness, pulled her close to him, and his lips came down slowly to warm hers. It was a provocative invitation to let him in. She opened her mouth, letting up his primal need to possess her. He devoured her lips, his tongue seducing her mouth, searching for hers in a dance that oozed with passion. Wet with the urgency of purpose, sensually riveting!

Their bodies molded as if one, his muscled thighs pressing down her soft curves, her toes tipped to reach his demanding lips finally, his strong hands lifting her up! A poignant beauty caught in their memory to paint!

Jasmine was moved by the possessive quality of his rugged strength, alive with raw sexuality and the sophistication of his indomitable power to take her. She felt unadulterated joy, an emotion evoked by the prospect of being possessed by him completely, and felt the heat exploding within.

He was in a drunken stupor, trying to contain the disquieting sexual desire that had long lain dormant inside of him. "I don't know how long I can endure wanting you, how I can quench the temptation to possess you completely." He whispered to her while kissing the lobe of her ear.

He finally loosened his tight embrace and looked passionately into her eyes, searching for an answer to his question, how could he pacify the consuming desire. They were both over the moon in love, and they had just realized the force that was hitting them harder as the days passed by. Zach was never demonstrative of his emotions when it came to desire or affection for a woman, but with Jasmine, he was powerless to the pervasive and voracious appetite to take and possess her.

After taking a deep breath, he composed himself and took her hand, kissing it, saying unapologetically, "My heart beats, and my mind makes me do things that my body demands to calm my desire for you, and the nearness of you always evokes those actions." He gave her a warm smile and a quick brush of his lips on hers. And off they went out of her place.

"Welcome to my place. I'll give you a quick tour before dinner is ready." Zach said as he ushered her inside and closed the door behind them. Julie, who was there in the living room waiting for them, was demure and radiant as the hostess. She extended her hand to Jasmine without waiting for Zach to introduce her, "I'm Julie. Nice to finally meet you, Jasmine," And gave Jasmine a quick welcoming hug.

"Pleased to meet you, Julie, finally seeing for myself how pleasant and lovely you are." Jasmine mused while giving her an unassuming smile.

"Thank you, please make yourself comfortable, and I'll see about our dinner. It must be ready by now!" She walked away after giving Zach a peck on his cheek.

That was not acceptable to Jasmine's little conscience, experiencing again that calculating sense, assessing Julie's lack of compunction. But, of course, she could not discuss any of it with Zach, who looked very devoted, completely taken, and besotted by Julie's persona. There was a lot for her to discover about Julie's true identity and her true relationship with Zach.

Zach never offered any explanation about his involvement nor cleared any doubts Jasmine was entertaining in her mind. Alright, Zach and Julie were not engaged. They were not lovers, but had he fallen in love with her, no matter how cavalier his reasons were in getting her to live with him? She was careful not to ask any questions or let her emotions take control and wreak havoc. She sat tightly, not letting out her doubts to show. Nevertheless, the thought came to her, had she been out of the equation, wouldn't Zach and Julie have been the perfect match to be lovers? Only the inevitability of her presence prevented and marred that possibility!

The dinner, helped by Julie, was superb. She had the domestic quality sought by men, the beauty that could behold them, and the vibrant quality her youth offered.

Zach was proud of her and was responsive to her demonstrative nature, her customary endearment holding and tapping Zach's hand or shoulder, her fluttery glances, and pecking! Either she was playacting her ulterior motives, or she was naturally loving and caring altogether. Zach's joy in living with her and loving her company was obvious!

"Zach is letting me go to Santa Barbara with my classmates during the spring break. Isn't he a wonderful brother!" And she turned to Zach and kissed him on his cheek. "I wonder where he'll send me after my graduation, and of course, he knows my obsession with Paris, France! I offered to work part-time with you guys to partly pay for my expenses, but he refused to even touch the subject with a ten-foot pole!" She giggled demurely, and Zach just smiled at her childish demeanor.

"That's a good idea. You'll get a clear perspective on what kind of work really interests you when you venture out to work. Why not, Zach? I'm sure you can't clip her wings and be very protective of her. When she's ready to soar, she'll go!" Jasmine said.

"Maybe he doesn't trust me enough about men. He's afraid I might fall into the wrong hands of a dishonest beguiling Romeo. My protective brother, may his soul rest in peace, would never haunt you. You have surpassed the kindness and goodness anybody would expect to give to an orphan like me. You have provided me a good home, paid for all my expenses, and mostly, made me feel loved and experienced having a family, though adoptive, but any good one would pale in comparison to yours." Julie summarized her life.

She stood up, raised her glass, and made a toast, "To you, Zach, you're the best, a friend and a brother in spirits and in deeds. May your gentle love and kindness flourish forever. I love you and owe you a lot. You made me the kind of person I am now. My brother, especially, is looking down on us, happiest for leaving me in your care. Thank you so much!" And tears of joy fell from her lovely hazel eyes.

Jasmine was also teary, a bit embarrassed for thinking so little of her. She was moved when she saw Zach taking Julie in his arms, wiping her tears, kissing her eyes, and gazing lovingly at her. The tenderness was caught in that one moment in time. Jasmine now understood the connection between the man she loved and the adopted sister he took in his care. He loved and nurtured her until she would be ready to be on her own. Witnessing it all gave her the poignant story of Zach's secret that she would cherish in her heart, devoid of doubts and distrust.

Jasmine raised her glass, toasting the two people before her, "To you, Zach, for being the most generous and loving person that you are, and to you, Julie, luckiest that your life got entwined with his, may the two of you have the best of everything and enjoy your made in heaven friendship and relationship, long live!" And glasses were clinked, smiles were exchanged, and serene happiness was evident.

It was Zach's time to say what he had wished for in a long while. He raised his glass and said, "To Jasmine, you're the love of my life then and now, thank you for allowing me to grace your life again, and to you, Julie, when your wings are ready to soar, Jasmine and I will be there to give you the boost and will always welcome you in our lives." And once more, their glasses clinked, and their lives had taken on a better turn.

Jasmine got ready to leave and said goodbye to Julie. In a lighter and happier way, they gave each other a hug and a silent prayer for their spirits, looking forward to a warmer and loving connection in the future.

Zach was quiet, engrossed in his driving. His mind had certain things on a loop. One, a big thorn was extracted from his heart, having cleared his connection to Julie, without a single word from him, eloquently explained by Julie's toast. It cleared Jasmine's mind about the true nature of his relationship with Julie. The second toast was a subtle hint of wanting her in his life, and thirdly, the thought-engaging thing was his restless desire to be intimate with Jasmine to quell his hunger for her love and closeness.

No matter how amorous he felt, how respectable his intentions were and how strong his feelings for her were, he was always in awe. Jasmine, with her bruised ego and diminished confidence in her sexuality, was a big hurdle for him to overcome.

He knew Jasmine would not make a move or show her sheer anticipation and willingness to try anything. She would lay in wait for him to initiate what he had been craving to do. Just like the morning coffee break they shared, she asked for a very discreet way of meeting or treating each other. She wanted to still keep her distance. It was not the way he wanted to treat her every time they saw or worked together. He wanted to draw her near to smell her scent and bury the worries of her life. He wanted to kiss her sweet lips and feel the rapture of a promising relationship.

"You have been very quiet. What are you thinking about?" She asked when they were just a few blocks from her place. Don't miss the turn on the next block." She gave a sweet chuckle that stirred a tingle on Zach's groin, and his mind went back to the most sensuous predicament now on his mind.

"Here's the turn. I won't miss it." And he drove his car in, alighted, and went around to open the car door for Jasmine. Instead of saying goodbye, he took her elbow and led her to the house. She opened the door, and he did not wait for an invitation from Jasmine.

He stepped in and walked straight to the fridge taking out a bottle of beer leftover from their weekend barbecue. He took a sip and stood by the counter, looking at Jasmine with dangerous hawkeyed precision. Ready for the kill in a slow but intense sexual predatory way.

Jasmine had seen that familiar appealing sexy stance but not with that kind of look. Something seemingly dangerous and primitive was burning in those blue eyes. His mesmerizing gaze conveyed a raw and untamed sensual signal. She was a little alarmed but thrilled, confusedly aroused by an unknown force from her gut. Immediately recognizing the peculiar burning passion that he had displayed before he left her that one evening.

Was she ready to experience another torrid encounter with him? What if she could not control her own desires, emotions, and decisions? What if he'd lost grip of his own sexuality? Were they ready for it, even though they were consenting adults and very much in love?

She took off her coat, discarded her three-inch heeled shoes, barefoot at five foot five inches. She walked towards him boldly, looking straight into his intense blue eyes, waiting for words to come out of his provocative mouth instead of the stench of beer.

She tugged his shirt and said, "What's eating you up, Zach? You have been very quiet, even at that nice dinner we had with Julie, which had turned out to be enlightening, especially to me. It made me understand your circumstances in life."

"It's about you, Jasmine. You've become an enigma to me. I'm losing sleep over the complexity you're transforming to be before my very eyes." He said, returning her searching gaze very seductively. He wanted to crush her lips against his at this very moment. And he inwardly wished for her to throw herself into his arms with the same fire burning within him.

"Why would I become an enigma to you, Zach?" Her voice was sultry, almost velvety. She was playing her own game, enticing Zach to get lost in her sensuality. They both knew that touch, no matter how light would propel them both to a stupor-like enchantment, igniting the fire and ravishing them both, there would be no turning back!

She struggled to feel unaffected by his fiery gaze, though she wanted him badly, more than she was letting on. He knew the moment they touched, he would be lost in a swirling pool of passion, his blood boiling, desire shooting through him, urging him to bask in the bosom of her sensuality and to take her completely to paradise!

Taking his time before being consumed, the memory of last night's passionate kisses couldn't hold a candle to the real thing now happening, the urgency of his potent need that overruled every ounce of common sense he possessed, fighting hard to erase the sting of being celibate for a long while in his life, driving him to the edge every time he was alone with her, like tonight, she was his for the taking, absolute acquisition, a trophy to his dreams!

"An enigma you are. One moment you're right here on my palm, your lips on mine. Next time, your mind is miles away, spanning a great distance between us. What is it that you really want, Jazz?"

"A thing that I can't have and possess right now! You matter to me, Zach, more than you'll ever know, more than I can comprehend, but life has its perplexities, some beyond my reach. At times, it's better to live on the status quo than venture out seeking the unknown without the certainty of the future. Like it's better to have loved and lost than never to have loved at all, at least, the pain would subside somehow. Whereas at the moment, complexities are confronting me, a nameless desire is forcing me to be possessed by you, its heat scorching my very soul. If I didn't taste it, I would die not knowing the ecstasy of your love. That I can't bear to take!"

"Jazz, never look at the glass half empty, be optimistic! There is no retreat from love. There is only sweet surrender. You have to be unfeeling or dead for not grabbing even a thin thread of possibility to feel love again, even our kind of love in the past, resurrected. I'm here for you, no less but more, the same person whose soul was lost before. Now warm-blooded with love for you! Please take me back, trust me again, and give me the breath of life I need to make you feel loved and appreciated. Do not punish us both by withdrawing your compassion and denying us the chance to be happy. We can have it all. It's our time to celebrate our love! Would you allow me to grace your life and try again?"

He moved towards her, she stepped back, and their eyes locked in anticipation. He extended his hand, imploring her to make the connection. The touch that could ignite the dying embers, light the way, and imbue the only breath needed to sustain them. He kept moving, one little step at a time. It made time stand still, went a decade back, his hand still reaching for her love and mercy until he felt a warmth that radiated from her breath. When he opened his eyes, her face was a kiss away.

He held her in rapturous joy. They gazed at each other. She looked down to reach for his hand, and the connection was made. For a while, they stood there in wait, both wondering what could happen between them, until Jasmine tagged his hand and led him to the couch, saying in a softer tone that sitting together would ease any perceived burden between them.

He kissed her hand, and they both sat, holding each other. He held her face with both his hands and kissed her asking, "What now, Jazz? You have heard everything I needed to say, and I'm waiting for your affirmation on the solutions to things that are now confronting us. I never wanted to pressure you, do take your time. I have been waiting patiently. What's more to do?"

"I know, and I appreciate your patience in very considerate and loving ways. I wish I could just say yes to everything you want. We're adults, but our lives should not only be concerned with our feelings and desires. There's a lot on your plate, and I need to know how you'll resolve it!"

"We're both accomplished in our line of work and have mostly gone past all the inconveniences in our lives. Why can't we move on to something that would give us joy and wholesomeness, like making love to you whenever I want to, unless I'm not the one you want, is there someone else?" A bit doubtful, he shook his head and gazed at her beautiful brown eyes.

"Zach, you know there's no one in my life but you. I liked you then, and I like you now more than ever, but there are other things I have to deal with."

"Liking is not the same as loving! I like girls. It doesn't mean I love them!" He was not being facetious, but he wanted to come across without showing his hurt. And to his dismay, nothing was really coming across to her, except the memory of her hurt feelings from a long time ago! He was getting afraid he was losing his patience.

"I fully understand where you stand on matters of the heart, have it your way. I can't prevail upon you to do my bidding. You do as you please. I take it, mine gets the least priority, and other things take precedence in your life." He did not get the commitment he wanted from her. He stood up and went to the door, said his goodbye and was gone! It left Jasmine berated, plastered, and speechless, but her pride was greater! She did not know how to say yes to Zach!

Life at work went on without any hitch from either of them. They were both courteous and respectful. Hard work was the only way to make the hours pass by. Zach, desperate with the situation, tried his best to keep his distance in a more acceptable way, going out to meet clients and engaging in different meetings with other department heads, doing all the work that he had set aside to make the time. Jasmine was indecisive. His efforts were futile, still naught.

"Hello, miss beautiful. I'm glad you're home early." Suzy was on the phone reminding Jasmine about Saturday night, her birthday.

"Don't worry about driving down here. I'll pick you up, or Jasper. Be ready at 7 pm. I'm busy, so I have to go, just be gorgeous as always, and break some legs! Okay? Bye." And she hung up without the usual talk.

At Suzy's, the place was decorated with plenty of colorful lights, people milling around, and good music softly playing. The gathering started at 6 pm, and Suzy, being the celebrant, was going around talking to friends and introducing new friends. She was glad Zach came in at 6:30 pm with Julie, very beautiful in her pink dress that emphasized her slim body curves and her youth, her arm clinging to Zach as if telling everyone he was hers alone.

"Looks like your best friend is not here yet." Zach looked around, referring to Jasmine as he talked to Suzy.

"Oh, Jasmine will be here a little after 7. I asked Liam to pick her up because Jasper was busy with other visitors from San Francisco." Suzy told Zach as she waved her hand to another friend.

"Food is ready, please help yourself, and I reserved a place for you and Jasmine over there," She pointed to a corner table near the dancefloor, and then she left.

Zach felt a little uncomfortable knowing that Jasmine was picked up by Suzy's friend when he could have gone by her house to pick her up, not minding Julie with him since the two had already met before and were friendly with each other. But it was not his party, and decisions were not made by him. After a little talk with another acquaintance, Zach went to the table assigned to them where he could view the whole garden, to watch dancing couples and new people coming in. He left Julie to get some drinks, then sat comfortably beside her, looking around for familiar faces working in the same business or involved in the kind of work he was engaged in.

Zach saw heads turn when Jasmine, very classy and attractive, came through the open sliding doors, onto the garden, with her hand possessively clinging to the arm of a tall, handsome guy looking proud, escorting an elegantly dressed woman and casually waving to some old friends. They were met by the celebrant, Suzy, who brought them to Zach's table and conscientiously introduced Liam.

"Zach, this is Liam, Jasper's friend, and associate, whom I asked to pick Jasmine up because Jasper went out to get other visitors from our hometown. Liam, this is Zach and her little sister, Julie. Zach is Jasmine's boss where she works."

"Liam Simons, pleased to meet you, Zach." He extended his hand to Zach for a handshake as he looked at Julie.

"Likewise, I'm Zachary Jennings, and this is my sister Julie." He turned to Julie as he introduced Liam to her. Jasmine was watching the two guys as they shook hands, hoping Zach was not slighted with the idea of Liam picking her up.

"The pleasure is mine, Miss Julie," Liam said as he smiled at her and continued to gaze into those beautiful, mischievous eyes of hers.

"Hi, Liam, nice to meet you. Suzy's friend is our friend!" Julie said as she happily and meticulously contemplated Liam's good looks and wholesome personality. It looked as though the intro was casual, but to two people whose chemistry was obvious, the slightest vibe was heartfelt.

It did not bother Liam, but he listened carefully to his feelings. Julie seemed very young, but she had displayed the finesse of a sensually conscious person in spite of her young age. She could easily grow up and transform into a sensuous woman just like what he saw in Jasmine, and now his plight with Jasmine became blurry because of what he had learned about her and Zach, which was just a scratch on the surface. There were so many things to learn about her, about them. Surely, Julie would provide a good intermission, a pacifier for his heart, which was getting restless. He pulled the chair next to him and offered it to Jasmine, across from Zach, who was seated next to Julie.

After the introduction, Liam leaned toward Jasmine, who was looking at him, trying to figure out the mood between Zach and him at the moment. She knew that Zach was not pleased with her in the arms of a stranger, a very handsome stranger!

Was Suzy seriously bent on pairing Liam by introducing him to Julie to stir Zach's attention from Julie to Jasmine? Jasmine was attracted to Liam, but her heart belonged to Zach. No one else could make her feel the way Zach made her feel. In her lifetime, no one ever touched her soul the way he did, and no one would compare to him. Liam, though, was a different kind!

After the meal, people engaged themselves in little talk with whomever they knew before or newly met. Some went dancing. Julie took Zach's arm, and they danced with a light beat. Liam took Jasmine and danced farther from the two, so he could have her to himself, away from the penetrating eyes of Zach.

Every once in a while, Zach's eyes went looking for them. As the music changed to a sweet love song, Liam did not let go of Jasmine. Zach was jealous, looking at Liam closely dancing with Jasmine, who was trying her best to avoid his gaze, concentrating on the comforts of Liam's strong arms. The instant she looked his way, Zach was contemplating, their eyes locked in an intimate moment. Everyone at the party disappeared, and they were alone in their own world! Zach's cell phone rang, and his contemplation was interrupted, and he answered the call.

"Oh, hello, Steve, what's up, any of the big jobs in trouble? Yeah, there are new changes made to accommodate the selection of different parameters to run specific reports. I'm here at a party with Jasmine. Let me get her to talk to you, hold on." He looked and signaled at Jasmine to come back to the table, pointing at his cell. When Jasmine approached

Zach, he said, "Steve is on the phone to talk to you." He gave his cell to Jasmine and went to talk to Julie. Explained to her about the sudden work call for them.

"Julie, would you like me to drop you off home, or would you prefer to stay and have Suzy take you home later?" Zach directed his attention to Julie.

"I'm staying, just starting to enjoy the party. Liam is here. He can take me home later." Julie told Zach and added, "I'll be home safe. Don't you worry, go and resolve the problem at your work. I know my curfew time, and you'll surely call to make sure I made it home safely. Right?"

Looking at Liam, he said, "I guess we have to exchange partners. Would you be kind enough to take my sister home? I'll get Jasmine home after we finish our job at the office?"

"Sure, I'll do that for Julie." Then Liam looked at Jasmine and said to her, "Sorry about work. Zach will take you home. I'll call you tomorrow. Take good care of yourself."

Zach referred back to Julie and said, "Of course, you know the drill. Bye." He signaled Jasmine to go with him and said their goodbyes to the rest.

"I'll take Jasmine home, Suzy. Liam promised to drive Julie home. Okay? Thanks, and good night." He drove to work with Jasmine by his side.

At work, Steve laid out the problems why the computer job bombed out, and since he could not get hold of the programmer who could troubleshoot minor problems, he was sorry to interrupt the merry partying of Zach and Jasmine.

They started to diagnose the error and went to work. Jasmine made sure the correct parameters were used to match the date and the requested reports. She had to check the input submitted by the client, as well as the changes made by the quality control clerk, and she made sure the updated Master tape was submitted to run the job, which was confirmed by Steve.

"Need any help from me? Steve showed me the error codes generated, and you got it right. It was the wrong parameter selected that caused the job to blow up. After your correction, the rerun would take more than two hours to see it past the point where it blew up, so we have to wait a while." Zach was saying to Jasmine, wondering if she was pissed off because of the error that cut off her time with Liam.

"Sorry, your good time with Liam was cut short," A twinge of jealousy could be sensed in his voice.

"No problem, we might as well wait for the whole job to run. In case any other part of the job would be affected by the change in a parameter, we might as well wait for the recap produced if the figures are balancing out with the total amount given to us. That would be another hour and a half to complete the run."

"That decision is fine with me. Let me tell Steve. We'll be at my office waiting." He went to tell Steve that they would be at his office working on other things while waiting to complete the job run, so they did not have to come early in the morning to check on the figures before running the final reports.

Up they went to the third floor, Zach switched on the lights and said to Jasmine, "Make yourself comfortable. Feel free to switch on my computer if you need to check on other things while we're here waiting." He went to his office fridge and checked what he could offer to Jasmine. Anything to eat or drink, definitely not coffee. Maybe decaf tea would be acceptable. "Want tea or soda?"

"Hot tea is fine. It was too cold in the computer room. I wonder how Steve is able to manage working there alone in that freezing cold condition!" She said as she sat on Zach's chair, feeling comfortable, and as her back touched the warm upholstery, she thought of the comfort his arms could possibly offer while the masculine scent of his aftershave lotion still lingered around her, titillating her senses. She quietly sniffed the pervading smell around her. It was all of Zach's masculinity that lived in her memory.

She was reflecting on her feelings for him when he reappeared, bringing two cups of hot tea. "You're in deep thoughts. It seems far away. Where to? Not with Liam, I hope!"

Feeling a little embarrassed, she could have told him the naked truth that she was daydreaming, not of Liam but about him.

"Oh, just random thoughts! That's all, nothing in particular!" She looked at him in a tender way, the way she was feeling at the moment. It's because of her pride, yes, foolish pride, that kept the happiness away from her.

"*I would like to be included in those random thoughts, more than you'd care to know! You are always in mine!*" He thought as he sat in front of his desk, looking straight at her.

"We have time to talk about us right here, personal not related to work. May we? Please do not offer any excuse. This is an opportune time to resolve our many issues." He reached for her hand, and Jasmine looked at his hand, holding hers tenderly. She did not have the courage to deny him the privilege.

"I may not have been vocal and demonstrative of my feelings for you, but let me make it clear that I loved you then, although I never said so, and I love you now more than I could ever express. Please listen and believe me!"

"I would be lying if I told you that I knew nothing about how you feel. Your gaze and your demeanor speak a thousand words of love. It's me who's in denial because of my foolish pride and misconception of your present circumstances."

"And what do you think is not acceptable about my present circumstances?" Zach asked, a bit in consternation but guessed. "Is it about Julie in my life?"

"Now that I'm aware of your relationship and having met her, it has lessened the worries. Nevertheless, your relationship with Julie affects your ability to totally connect with another person, let alone be completely affectionate without regard and consideration of her."

"Are you jealous of her? Do you think my heart does not totally belong to you, that a part of me belongs to her? That's the biggest nonsense bull I've ever heard, and coming from a highly intelligent person like you, it's inconceivable! Be real. Snap out of it! I won't take any of that!"

"Would you rather have me unaffected by competition? Would you want me to share you with somebody else, one who's always loving, touching, and kissing you on any given occasion?" Jasmine dared Zach to answer her straightforwardly with the barest truth in his answers.

"No, of course not. But Julie is not a lover, not a competitor but an adopted sister who still needs guidance and care. Not in any romantic inclination! You own my heart, my body, and soul, and I want only you and no one else in this world. Why can I not imprint that in your soul?"

"You want me to believe and accept that, but my heart is still wary of losing you again. I live in fear, and if you ever desert me again, I know I won't survive."

"I promise you that will never happen. If you like, we could start living together in your place, and we'll just check on Julie for her needs until she can be on her own. After that, can we properly plan out our life together and have a family?"

She contemplated that offer. It was not a marriage proposal, just a kind of offer to live together, and after Julie was gone, he would do the proper thing to plan their life together and have a family.

"You know I'm bound by strict morality. That does not allow me to live with you even if we're in a loving relationship. Yes, we could be lovers, and we could kiss here and there, but that's about it, only promises no commitment!"

"You're living in the past, in the medieval ages! Grow up and look around you. We'll not be living in sin. We're just buying time! I'm a bit worried about how you look at things these days. Tell me, Jazz, what do you really want me to do? I'm done guessing." He looked at her, searching the state where her mind was set.

"It's not for me to ask. You're the captain, the navigator. Don't you really know what I want?" She showed exasperation. She knew what she wanted from him, yet, she could not say so, afraid of repercussions or fear that it might alienate him.

"Every time I try to understand you, the more I'm puzzled as to what I should do or offer. It seems my love and promises are not enough. I can't plan our future without first coming to an understanding of how and where we're truly at. I know we can't get married yet, that takes a lot of consideration and planning, but we'll get there." He stood up and went to the table to pick up some papers and went back to her, waiting for a response from her.

"Are you intending to marry me in the future?" She bravely asked, straight to his face, with no more preamble. "If so, why can't you propose? Then, we can just talk about all the problems that are preventing the marriage, like your preoccupation with Julie's future."

"I know that's the uppermost detriment in your mind, although it's not my preoccupation or my priority either. I can deal with that on the side, believe me. What bothers me is my inability to grasp your mental state. Like you're afraid of things, you have premonitions that are weighing down on our interactions with each other. I can't even go near you to hold and caress you. It's driving me crazy, not knowing what's going on in that beautiful head of yours."

"Nothing's going on in my head. What I fear is real. It's uncertainty!" She said without elaborating.

"What uncertainty? About the future? Do I need to propose to you now so that it would lessen some of our worries? Can I not choose the proper occasion and the right time? You know the pressure is not a good tool to make me perform. The more pressure there is, the more resistance I give. I want to do things the way I want them done at my own choosing, at my own bidding." He did not offer any other explanation and stopped asking her questions when he saw the time on his watch.

Zach ended his discussion with Jasmine when he saw it was time to check on Julie. He needed to know if Julie had finally made it home. He called her on his cell, "Julie, where are you right now? Who took you home?" He was anxious to know who had taken her home.

"Zach, I'm home right now, and not to worry, Liam took me home, and yes, you don't need to ask. He is a perfect gentleman! Actually, we just made it to the door. What? Do you want to talk to him? Here." Julie gave the phone to Liam and said, "Here, my eccentric brother wants to talk to you."

"Hi, Zach, yeah, we've made it here. Everything is alright. I'll make sure she's inside and all locked up. Don't worry, your sister, no matter how young, is amazingly good-natured and highly responsible." After getting assurance from Liam, Zach thanked him and talked to Julie again, then hung up his phone.

After the quick assuring talk with Zach, Julie told Liam, "Come inside. Would you care for some hot tea before you go? It will be nice to have a quiet talk here instead of the noisy place at the party. You said you want to know more about me." Julie smiled.

That was the cue. Liam wanted to ask about the circumstances that led her to get involved in Zach's life. He also wanted to know the real consequence of Zach's relationship with Jasmine. At that given point in time, Liam was confused about the relationship between Zach and the two beautiful and attractive women whom he came to meet in just a short time. He wanted to understand the theory behind the intriguing trio.

He liked Jasmine. She was an attractive person, discreet, a little mysterious, and private. At the same time, Julie is a lot younger and awesomely beautiful but has not acquired the kind of maturity, sensuality, and elegance of Jasmine in comparing the two women. If given a choice, Liam was more interested in wanting to know more about Jasmine, whom he perceived as an epitome of womanly love and sexuality. He was more fascinated by maturity, sophistication, and responsibility in women than in the enthusiasm or the sheer excitement of the young and immature.

But Julie seemed different from other young and unapologetic women of the new generation. She displayed a cool attitude, understanding, and broader grasp of life itself, not naughty but nice, well-bred and educated, and not spoiled or selfish. Zach had a lot to do with her good upbringing even though he came later into her life just a few years ago, since her biological brother died, who also did a good job of bringing her up as an orphan sister.

It was a bit early for Liam to know about his true feelings for the women in his life, the two new women he had just met, and his previous choice Suzy. They all seemed to be taking part in his love life. Suzy was foremost in his mind. He had secretly been fascinated with Jasper's little sister, even when she was only twelve years young and barely conscious of sexuality. Liam was eighteen then, the time he met Suzy, introduced by her brother Jasper.

From Zach's house, Liam went back to Suzy's house, happily helping her clear the place up to the wee hours of the morning. He had free access to the house and had a designated room in the household, and was always welcome to stay there even when Jasper was not there.

Although he was not too comfortable staying when Suzy was alone, he was afraid his feelings for her would surface, which could harm or compromise her refutation with other people. Sometimes he slept at his office, but other times in the house where he kept his things.

Julie was honest and open about herself, baring her soul to Liam, the first man in her life who had touched her heart romantically and made her aware of her own womanhood and her capacity to acknowledge love. She liked Liam a lot, in spite of their difference in age. She was already beginning to fantasize about having a love relationship with him, should he continue to see her in the future.

She was also truthful about Zach and Jasmine's circumstances and what she knew about the complications in their relationship, their history in the past, and their known present predicaments that seemed to mar the smooth transition from the past life to the present. And she knew she was a contributing factor to the known complications, but she was helpless to alter the situation, nor would she intrude on their personal difficulties.

Back at the office, Zach sat in front of Jasmine to face another hurdle, another onslaught to his train of thoughts. Looking glum, he decided to finish work and no further discussion of anything about them, wishing it would be resolved sooner or later.

Jasmine understood that that was the end of any discussion about themselves, and it was time to go home. The drive home was drab and painstakingly slow. It was so like him to prove his point, but Jasmine was equally stubborn to follow her instinct and never gave up on what she aimed for. If he truly loved her and wanted her badly, he had to show it and make a commitment, which she knew would not come any sooner, not yet, but hopefully in the future.

He drove the car into Jasmine's driveway and alighted, opened the car door for Jasmine, and followed her inside the house. She did not say a word nor asked any question and assumed he would stay a while, probably to talk her into his own preferred way of dealing with the problems that were confronting them.

"There is food in the fridge. Would you like to eat?" She asked solicitously, but Zach's mood was unabashed. He went to her room and used the bathroom. When he came out, he had taken off his clothes and was just wearing shorts and a cotton shirt, ready to sleep on the couch.

"It's past two in the morning. You don't mind me sleeping here on the couch? If I may, please have a pillow and a warmer sheet. I suddenly feel very tired and sleepy. It's not wise to go and drive home." He sat on the sofa and took off his shoes while Jasmine was looking at him, not believing how casual and cold he was treating her. She went to her bedroom to pick up the requested beddings.

"Here are two pillows and a light comforter and some slippers- the floor is cold." She fixed the couch to make it nice and cozy, and all she got was a cold thank you from him. He lay down and said, "Good night."

She went around to make sure all the doors were closed and set the alarm and provided him with a night light at the corner of the sofa in case he wanted to get up and find his way to the bathroom. After saying, "Good night, sleep well," she left her bedroom door unlocked because she trusted him, especially when his mood was as drab as the night before, which stripped him of his desire to make love to her.

He knew she was bothered by his silence, but he could only state his case not in so many ways, and for some time, he was running short of his own fuse. He felt tired of begging her to understand his situation. She knew he needed her, but she chose to ignore his desire and longings for her. Would she ever listen to her own need for his closeness or bury her head under the sand and ignore his pleading to understand his needs for intimacy and love from her? Both their strategies were not working, and rather, the rift was getting deeper and more complicated. Neither one wanted to compromise nor beg! Hence, they both suffered in vain!

It was almost 9:30 in the morning when he woke up. At first, he was unsure where he was, but when he heard Jasmine from the kitchen, he remembered what had transpired the night before. "Would you care for a cup of brewed coffee the way you like it?" Jasmine asked softly, her voice with a little tenderness, but it did not move the needle far enough to appease the growing dissatisfaction from Zach's hurt feelings.

"Yes, please. Thank you. It'll be a minute- get to dress up and be gone before you know it." He stood up and headed to her bedroom to retrieve his clothes and use the bathroom. He appeared after a few minutes, fully dressed, and took the cup of coffee she offered. He said to her, "Thank you, this will wake me up. I'll pass by the office, check on Steve and see if everything is okay. You don't need to come that early tomorrow; I'll pick up the recap and figures from the computer run, the ones I would need for Monday's report."

"You don't want me to go with you? Are you sure?" She was becoming more concerned with his cold display of disinterest in her company all of a sudden. He used to demand her tagging along with him every which way he went before.

"No, there's no need for that." He finished his coffee and headed to the door, then looked back at her following him. "Thanks for the accommodation last night. I was really tired. Bye." He headed to his car without another word, not even a quick glance at her, waiting at the door, seeing him off. He drove off without giving her a look or a wave, evident that he was truly pissed off about what was going on in their relationship.

Jasmine waited for his call for an update at work, but no call from him came through the whole afternoon. She did not want to complicate matters, intrude further or spoil his quiet evening with Julie, as she had pictured them to be enjoying their day together. She felt the pang of jealousy grip her heart. That was the reason why Zach could not commit his love to her. It was indeed a concern for Julie's welfare and presence in his personal life. Julie was first, and she was only second to Zach's priorities! She could not accept nor tolerate that, not with his love. She would rather wallow in despair, unhappiness and loneliness than share his love with another woman, be her an adopted sister or whatever!

Jasmine was in that desolate mood when her phone rang. It was Liam calling. "Hi, Liam, just the right person I want to talk to! How are you since the party?"

"Just fine, thank you, and how about you?" Liam happily interjected, sensing Jasmine's feat way of hiding her true mood. "You're not really feeling as gaily as you try to sound, are you? Care to tell me? Or maybe you need my loving arms around you to calm down any raw nerves throbbing in that beautiful head of yours?"

"Liam, I know how perceptive and intuitive you are. You don't even know me, and yet you seem to grasp what's going on in my midst. I don't want to burden you with my nonsense predicaments." Jasmine offered him a reason instead- she was not ready to discuss and scare away Liam from her dreadful thoughts and worries. He did not deserve to worry about her, and she needed to give him better treatment, a friendship from her that she knew she was capable of giving him. "Let's instead learn more about each other, the good first rather than the ugly truth, won't you agree?"

"Of course, that's why I keep calling. I want to know you better, to find what makes you tick and stir interest in people. But I also want to help, in case you need my shoulders to lean on, not wishing you to cry on, but nevertheless, I am willing and able to provide that too!" He, so eloquently, offered his helping hand for her to hold on to in times of uncertainty!

"Liam, Liam, thank you, maybe someday I will really need your advice, but before you can do that, you must first know me well." Jasmine was reminded of how complicated her life story with Zach was.

"I must be open and honest about what I know about you. I don't want to hide things from you. The moment I laid eyes on you, I felt you are the kind of person I like in life, in whatever capacity. I became aware of your involvement with Zach from close colleagues and friends about your history with him. I have no qualms about your previous relationship because I believe in your discretion, and if you think I'm entitled to know some things about your life, then I'm more than honored to celebrate that privilege." He profoundly stated his understanding of her.

"I don't want to hide from people whom I consider friends, but of course, I want my privacy kept to just a few. I'm willing to answer any of your queries, but I reserve the right to keep private other things that are intimate and personal." She offered him the opportunity to ask what he wanted to know about her.

"Are you and Zach engaged? Are you 100% tied up and in commitment with him? Is there a possibility someone special could steal your heart from him?" Liam asked in rapid succession, and her answers would either provide for the door to open or doomsday sealed.

"No, I'm not engaged to Zach and never was. There is no 100% foolproof. Each thing has even the slimmest possibility of ever happening or not happening. Yes, there is a saying that nothing is sure until it has already happened. Even married couples could eventually end in divorce!"

"I guess I got my answer there, thank you. I should never lose hope, aim, and strive for what I really want in life." Liam thought hard about the other things he wanted to know about Jasmine but kept quiet because she was very smart and did not give him any chance to get a definite answer from her, rather clouded with some ambiguity, the meaning depended on one's own interpretation.

"Did I make myself clear or made it more unfathomable to decipher the real meaning of it?" Was an engagement a deterrent? But if Liam's love was true, then that love must be worth fighting for!

"That's alright for the moment! Do you believe in love at first sight? Of soulmates?" He further tested Jasmine's own perception of true love.

"Yes, I do, to both your questions. Love comes in many forms- it comes naturally but can be taught to evolve and grow, flourishes when nurtured, dies when forsaken and abandoned, and others unsuitable and forbidden. So many stories, from being immortal to tragic. What kind of love do you want to have and feel, Liam?"

"One that is true, sweet, uncomplicated, and lasting!" He answered without hesitation, guile or deception. "How about you, Jasmine? If a man offers you respect, trust, constancy, and true love, will that satisfy you? All that and more, can that be enough to possibly win your restless heart? I know good looks alone will not hold the possibility to own your heart, and sometimes, love is not enough either!"

"Very true! Love is a complicated thing. It's mysterious and encompassing. It's more powerful than any forces on earth, it has many splendors, it has a soul, and it lives in the heart. It feels, it throbs, and it sings, but other times, it's sad, it whines and hurts!" Jasmine said, describing the many faces of love, bringing in either joy or tears, depending on one's circumstances!

"I think it has to be the kind of love we want to feel in our lives, the ways we look at it, the person we have chemistry with! And the kind of treatment we offer the object of our affection. If someone treats you shabbily, that person does not deserve your love and affection. Look for the kind, respectful and gracious people to become your friend, to know and grow with them. We all deserve to be treated the best. What you sow, you reap!" Liam said so eloquently!

"You are right, Liam. I think you already have an idea of the kind of woman you want in your life and the kind of love you're willing to share with her. I think she's a very special and deserving woman. Your looks, personal traits, and integrity, together with your amiable attitude, make you a perfect gentleman to own any lady's heart. After enjoying the acquaintance and company of Julie, did you find her a suitable lady for the most coveted place in your heart?"

"What made you think I was interested in Julie that way?" He, sort of, emitted a chuckle that did not go unnoticed by Jasmine. "Remember, I asked Suzy to meet you, to pick you up for her party, and I hung around until you were paired with Zach and I with Julie, and that party was where I first met them both. I did not choose to take her home, you went with Zach, and I was left with her, not both our choices. I was a gentleman, as the occasion called for!"

"Sorry for the mix-up and inconvenience. S... happens, you know!" She said, trying to subdue the laughter, afraid it might offend him. "But at least you had a chance to get closer to Julie and better get familiar and acquainted. Zach was very well protective of Julie, especially to a guy as good-looking and attractive as you are. You had the good chance that did not come along often. It could spell luck and fortune!"

"Really? Do you regard me as someone truly good-looking and attractive? That there is the possibility of winning a lady's heart and affection?"

"Of course you are! Even though beauty is subjective, there is no denying that your looks are truly amazing and whoever says you're not physically attractive is plain foolish, stupid, or blind! For me, your qualities are ubiquitously undeniable!"

"Wow, I feel elated and humbled- thank you, Jasmine, for that wonderful vote of confidence! You never cease to amaze me. You're not pulling my leg, or are you, just to make me feel better?"

"Nope, I always speak the truth, be it bare bone ugly or complimentary. In your case, it's the latter! Don't you have time to look at yourself in the mirror every morning, staring at the naked truth? Yes, Liam, you're handsome and very appealing! I'm sure there's a lot of women who look at you wishing your lips would crush theirs in hot kisses."

"Can I wish upon a star that you could possibly think of me that way, too? Or is it asking too much?"

"Who am I to ask you to stop wishing? We all wish every single day in our lives, don't we? That you're truly attractive, and sure you can win any lady's heart if you choose to pursue it! I think of you that way; there I said it! And, the only way you could lose is if someone already owned her love!" And in her thoughts, "*If I only could, wouldn't it be wonderful to feel happiness with you?*"

"I'll keep that in mind. Would you let me take you out to dinner on Tuesday night? I want to pick you up around 7:30- that way, you have enough time even if you finish work at 6 pm." Liam waited for her response accepting the date.

"Tuesday is fine, not too much work. All set then, so see you. Thanks for calling, and good night." They hung up, leaving them satisfied and happy about their phone conversation. However, at the thought of Zach, she felt guilty about encouraging Liam and accepting a date with him.

Part #3

It was time to dress up, remembering her date with Liam, who would pick her up by 7:30 that evening. She was thinking about Zach, who was still at the office when she left, and their relationship was still in status quo, and he was bent on letting it stay the way it was, consumed by itself! She was not happy about it, but at times it was better that way so that she did not have to worry about what came next.

Liam was prompt when he came to the door, gave her an orchid corsage, and greeted her with the most affable smile she so deserved after a long day of hard work, "Good evening, fair lady, are you ready to go?" He said while taking her hand to tuck it under his arms.

He took her to a warm and cozy place for an intimate dinner, evidently frequented by lovers. He chose a table at a dimly lit corner of the club, and the food was superb. She chose scampi shrimps smothered in butter and mussel soup garnished in ginger and other spices; additionally, they brought freshly baked bread with it. Liam selected roast beef with potatoes and veggies. White wine was their choice for their drinks. After dinner, dessert was served, a selection of special ice cream or creamy cheesecake.

The night was long and enchanting. Liam offered the comfort of his arms for her dancing pleasure. They were superbly matched looking at them as a couple; both were engaging and graceful, with the undeniable chemistry luster between them. They were both happy and enjoying each other's company. Jasmine was at peace, feeling warm and safe in the arms of Liam, who was as gentle and accommodating as any man would be dancing with the woman of his choice. At a glance, they looked like eager lovers, celebrating delightfully, dancing the night away under a starry sky lit by a blue moon!

"It's wonderful dancing with you, I hope it won't end!" Liam whispered in Jasmine's ear, thus waking her senses up, now aware of how close and intimate they were dancing. She did not disengage herself, thinking she deserved to feel this way and enjoy the moment. It was rare that she would dare to experience an emotion so raw and amorous. But, like a fawn that had stood on its legs for the first time, she was still trying to find reasons to explain her feelings, what made her react to him that way, she was powerless to shove him off and she felt totally under his spell.

She loved the way he looked at her and the way he touched her. At times, she daydreamed about him, wanting to hear his velvety voice, remembering the tenderness of his embrace and the sensuous feeling of his body against hers. It was like an awakening, confusing and mysterious, yet invigoratingly magical feeling.

She did not stay long at the office; when done with her usual work, she called Zach on the intercom and told him she was ready to leave and if there were any other matters he should take up with her. "Anything else you want me to do?"

"Yes, come and talk to me about what's going on with you, with us. Stop running away from me! I'm sick and tired of not knowing where I've gone wrong. Bring with you the new account file opened today!" He said with an exasperating tone.

That conversation with Zach made her anxious, now afraid of committing or accepting any offer from him. She needed total comprehension of her ambiguous feelings about Liam and Zach; she couldn't afford to be fickle-minded for long. She closed her door and headed to Zach's office, not knowing how she could explain to him what was truly in her mind. She knocked twice, opened the door, and found Zach seated behind his desk; she demurely entered and closed the door behind her.

She placed the requested file on his desk, looked at him solemnly, and said, "What do we need to talk about that we had not said to each other before?" She stood there, looking stern, not wanting to sit down to make the talk as short as possible.

"Sit down, Jasmine, unless you're in a hurry to meet again with Liam."

"What has Liam got to do with this, with us?" She bravely countered with her poker face, trying to appear unperturbed; she knew he was bluffing!

"Please tell me, you did not have dinner with Liam last night, and the two of you were not like love birds dancing the night away up to past midnight, grossly intimate and zealously romantic. Do I ever bluff or lie to you? I demand the same honesty from you, I deserve to know the truth. You're not leading me on a goose chase run, are you?"

"It was a harmless dinner date. Liam and I are just beginning to know each other. I have no commitment with you that would restrict me from seeing or dining with somebody else. Do I? It's not like I'm engaged to you that I'm no longer able to enjoy the company of male friends. I'm not a flirt!"

"How could you say that? Since you walked back into my life that fateful day, I never stopped making you feel wanted and loved. I made and took all my time apologizing for the grave mistake I made. What about our past and future? Aren't we just buying time to formalize our plans? I'm waiting to free myself from the responsibility restricting my commitment to you. I know Julie is the one that keeps us apart, a wedge in our relationship. I'm imploring you to please understand, and as soon as I'm free from that responsibility, I will start to plan our life together. You know I'm a person of few words and very private, and I know you are the most accommodating and reliable person I've known in my life, why would you turn your back on me now? Because I refused to disregard my commitment and overthrow my humanitarian deed on Julie?"

"You've never discussed anything with me, even about Julie, I learned bits and pieces here and there, but you never explained anything to me, in fact, you even evaded anything that had something to do about you and her. Like a big, dirty secret. What do you expect of me, Zach? To be emotionless, unaffected, and uncaring? To be there waiting for the time when you include me in your life. What should I do till then, no right or willpower to mingle with friends and feel alive while I wait for you to throw me a small bone of attention from time to time at your convenience?"

"It's not like that, you make me sound so horrible. I want us to be on our own, enjoy each other's company without any complications, and it's less than a year. As you know, Julie is graduating and will venture on her own with little or no help from me. Is it too much to ask for you to make a sacrifice for our future? Where is your compassion? Please reconsider where you stand on the matter; I need your moral support!"

"I'm considerate and compassionate, but I don't appreciate the guessing game! Between us, I prefer you to be unequivocal, direct, and explicit with no ambiguity or bull whatsoever!"

As she glared at him, putting her foot down for the first time, "Just like you, I'm not too vocal. I, too, relish privacy, so I don't like it when people know about my state of affairs better than I know myself! This mess could not have happened, had you put your faith in me and trusted me! I was always an outsider in your life, never allowed to even peep through the door! That was how you got away, without a word!"

"That's not true! I'm truly sorry, Jasmine. I thought keeping quiet would suffice, and eventually, things would get better! And for everyone's sake, happiness is just a few words spoken between us!"

"Oh, Zach, when would you learn to share your feelings, especially with me?" She rubbed her hands, her pretty head shaking, and her brown eyes filled with melancholia as they were focused at him.

"You never open up to me! Always tight-lipped!"

"I'm too jealous of Liam, I hardly could think. You never allowed me that close to you. I have longed to hold you in my arms for over a decade the way he did last night! There, I've told you how I truly felt! I hope you understand my craving for your love, affection and attention!" His soulful eyes locked with hers, imploring for understanding and forgiveness for his misgivings.

"I'm sorry, Zach, I did not know how you felt. I didn't mean to hurt you. To tell you the truth, I was exploring my own emotions, if sensuality had something to do with keeping the fibers of love burning in our hearts. I found that Liam was expressive, loving and caring, unafraid to show sensuality, and exploring his feelings for me. In the same way, I let him so that I could feel the same way with him. I was excited and found him respectable as we explored the new relationship we had created. With you, our relationship paled in comparison, vague, dreary, and indiscernible!"

"You are killing me; you explored your feelings with him while you always shunned me when I tried to make love to you. And now accusing me of being cold and indifferent?" He continued, upset and exasperated, "The more I tried to come closer to you, the more you imposed restrictions on our relationship; you forbid me from freely expressing how much I wanted you!"

"Love-making is sexual and different from exploring one's sensuality. What Liam and I did was real; I realized just how compatible we were. Not only physically but emotionally as well, but we did not go there, to that forbidden thing where lovers were allowed to venture and indulge. We did not neck, caress each other or even kiss! During those times, I thought about you. Why you could not be that way, loving, expressive, and sensuously engaging with me."

"I'm still jealous. You let him do that; you allowed him to stay and linger close to you for a long while. You never let me kiss you for more than a few moments, won't let me stay the night, to explore and enjoy all possibilities between us."

"Partly, because I'm afraid. Not of you, but of getting lost in your arms and kissing is a very dangerous thing, mind you! It was sort of a beginning of a courtship with Liam, shaping and molding it the way he wanted it. But with you, we have lost that stage, but you can't just grab and seal the deal or just hang the hat without holding, shaping, molding, and appreciating it to your liking!"

"I love you very much, Jasmine! I was afraid of how deep my feelings were for you and that I would lose myself. That was part of my mistaken perception, but now I'm not afraid to embrace the truth of how much you mean to me, that I wanted you from the day we met in high school and forever in my life." He went around his desk and took Jasmine in his arms, kissing her tenderly. His lips lingered longer than they had before, and more passionately, they were short of breath!

"Thank you for having the courage to profess your love for me! You don't know for how long I've dreamed of hearing it, ten years and going."

"I'm sorry, I thought I showed you how important you were in my life, then and now! Was that your reason for fidgeting all the way? You wanted the words spoken, recited, professed before you!" He continued kissing, pressing his hard body against her, his rigid manhood felt by Jasmine coming alive. His actions aroused her dormant desire for him to make love to her, she stood there without any complaint.

He interrupted his kiss and looked at her intensely before asking, "How am I doing? Am I getting better, sensuous, and demonstrative of my feelings for you?"

"I'm overwhelmed. You have to be threatened before you can express your desires. What about Liam? I don't need to explain everything to him, I was not leading him on just to get your attention. I have a dinner date with Liam next week, he deserves an explanation of why I can't see him anymore."

"Do that. Take it easy on him, I'm sure he would understand, there would be no hard feelings between us. But please, no intimate embrace and never kiss, your lips are mine and no other man should ever brush their lips on yours!"

He let her go and continued, "What about going to your place for dinner, a little cozy pillow talk, and maybe a dry run? Haven't we tried that yet? Get ready for me."

"Sure, I will. That sounds interesting, there's always a first! Pick up some food to go; I won't have time to cook!" She smiled, straightened her skirt, and walked to the door.

She said to him, "Bye, see you in 30 minutes or so at my place!"

Exactly after forty-five minutes, she arrived. The doorbell rang, and she saw Zach's car in her driveway, "Hello, again! Very prompt, thank you!"

She turned abruptly with the bag of food in her hands but was stopped short when Zach took her in his arms and gave her a lingering and passionate kiss. She almost dropped the food from her hands, "Whoa, that was earth-shattering, romantic and welcoming! Come inside, you must be starved."

"More love-starved than food starved, I want to eat a different meal tonight, if you allow me." She did not know whether he was kidding or insinuating another way of loving. He was bent on claiming his privilege over her; whatever it was, she had to stop dwelling on it in anticipation. So she moved to put the meal on the table and started eating with him!

"I know you love finger food, you can also try or be addicted to your lover's delight. I'll let you try that later, that would be the specialty for tonight. It's allowed for people to love each other and wait for the right time to get hitched. That's us!"

"Eat and enjoy the food. We have plenty of time to talk about other things!" She offered him drinks, and he chose to pick up the beer can that he had left at her place one afternoon.

After dinner, they went to her den, where the couch was bigger and wider, scattered with a myriad of cushions and throw pillows. The television was in the corner and the fireplace provided warmth from the smoldering logs. The air was permeated with the scent of wood, and the curtains were drawn down for privacy at night, but the higher glass windows were bare, giving a beautiful view of the night sky freckled with millions of stars. The place, time, and mood are all conducive to a session of explosive lovemaking, one that they have not done before!

"I like this part of your house, it's cozy and comfortable. The warmth of the place is always the perfect ambiance for a romantic evening like tonight. Would you care to watch the news with me and learn some tricks I'm willing to show and teach you?"

Zach pulled Jasmine's hand and let her sit next to him, his hold was firm and he knew what he planned to do. Make love to her, whether he would succeed without objection, but was willing to accept and compromise up to a point. Whether he was successful or not, at least he was trying to assert himself the way Jasmine wanted him to be, sexy, assertive, romantic and very courageous for at least trying!

"Would you care for another beer while we watch the news? I have some mixed nuts next to you there." She pointed to a can of nuts at the side table.

"You're not trying to make me drunk, if you are, then I'm not responsible for my actions!" Of course, he was kidding, probably wanting to prepare her for his unprecedented actions, he had already started to initiate his love process. He had waited for this moment, he had wanted to be intimate with Jasmine for a long time since that day she walked back into his life, he was holding back, not sure whether she was ready for it. He had been celibate all this time, wanting to offer her the glory of love-making between two people who truly cared for each other, them!

She gave him his second can of beer as she sat across him from the wide couch he had chosen. He motioned her to sit next to him, and when she did not budge, he stretched his arm, grabbed her and pulled her to sit next to him. They were sitting really close and he held her waist to prevent her from moving away from him and daringly stared at her, "What are you afraid of? My lips, my hands or just closeness? Isn't it time we get personally acquainted, at least in your place like now?"

"I just don't want you to get carried away, don't start something you can't finish." She said without looking at him. Was she challenging him or herself?

"Those days are gone. I'm ready for everything, from start to finish, please don't dare me to do just about anything between the two of us because you'll surely lose. Before I came down here tonight, I promised myself to do what I feel like doing, whether it conforms to good etiquette, logic, protocol, or norm, as long as it feels good for you and me. How's that for a change?"

"Quite daring and outlandish, unpredictable and unprecedented but possible!"

"Want to dare me to try or insinuate anything between a woman and a restless buck. It's worth the thrill!"

"You're in charge, and I dare not even slightly provoke any action from you. All or what you do is solely of your choosing, business, and responsibility!"

He curled her hair around his fingers, caressing her face, and touched her lips, "Are there areas I am supposed to explore, some restrictions, or things I should do or not do? Tell me, guide me, but please give me a free hand, for only then would you know if it feels good or not, unpleasant or so, but remember there's a very thin line between pain and pleasure! What is slightly painful or awkward to the inexperienced is tolerable and pleasant as we go along!"

He positioned himself in the most convenient way to be able to touch her, "I want you to relax and enjoy, feel the pleasure, joy, and rapture of being touched. Making love is giving and accepting pleasure from each other. Be submissive and feel the ecstasy that we could get and accept everything for its beauty, for the satisfaction we both could feel."

He stopped talking and let his hand work its way to caress her curves. He was not in a hurry, he had the whole night before him. He planned to stay the night without alarming her of his intentions.

Jasmine was anxious but did not show it, she was seeing another side of the man she had loved and valued in her life. She could not help but observe Zach; intrigue, suspense, and anxiety were the mixed emotions she was experiencing at the moment. It was entirely different from the ecstasy she felt with the subtle sensuality emanating from the virile masculinity of Liam, slow dancing with her, holding her tight, and brushing her temple with the warmth of his breath. It was more romantic and held her spellbound. She felt Liam was capable of exuding raw sexuality that cast the magic spell on her. How could she resolve the difference between her feelings for the two men who now had a significant role in her life?

With her growing anticipation of Liam's ability to steer her life in a different direction, she suddenly was obligated to consider Zach's confession and avowal, promising a big change in his dealings with Jasmine's feelings and resolving all their issues. Jasmine was considering which way she should tread, she was stuck at a crossroad. She could not see the purpose and peaceful coexistence in her love life.

If she chose to pursue a relationship with Liam, she was still uncertain what the future would look like because she had just met him a few weeks ago and was not sure if their personalities would be compatible in the long run. He was of age, educated, and stable in life with his own business. Additionally, he was tall, handsome, kind, and trustworthy. His magnetic charm and virile sexuality were part of the attraction that gave him the edge over her decade-long fascination with Zach's reserved, commanding, but strict and complacent nature. He was also very complicated partly by his mysterious hunger for closeness and obsession with privacy. She had found herself at a loss and pondering, unsure if her choice would be wiser, fruitful and beneficial.

Jasmine felt she needed more time, but Zach finally came to his senses, driven by the rivalry he had with Liam, and Zach was now putting pressure on her to accept him. Suddenly, Zach wanted some kind of closeness and intimacy with her, it scared the hell out of her! How should she sail and navigate the uncharted ocean of love to get the best choice of fish jumping all over her to catch. What if she made the wrong choice? Right now, she was blinded by the colorful and joyful emotions when she should accept the peaceful familiarity of the old feelings that had dominated her life. The value we assign to things correlating to our sense of belonging would be most valuable and enduring in life.

"I've been wondering about you. You seemed to be miles away and not here with me. Where are your thoughts, my love? Would you care to share them with me? Is it me or Liam on your mind? I would like to know?"

"Why would you think it's Liam on my mind and not you?" she wittingly fenced with him, "I'm always thinking of important things in life, like what you're up to, before you were too complacent and unresponsive to things that mattered to our relationship."

"Maybe it's the reconstruction of me, your former beloved is ongoing, and you're not too aware of it because of obstruction or preoccupation with newer things in your life? Like the matter of Liam on your mind, questioning, imagining things?"

"Don't talk in riddles, I rather you speak your mind directly, unambiguously and straightforward. Say what you mean and mean what you say." She was a little surprised at herself, how she could pull that manner of speaking in front of Zach. She was usually very careful not to disappoint or offend him, not in the most subtle way, even when she was very upset with him.

"Whoa! Is that the Chili Pepper kind of response I'm getting from you? It's not every day that we discuss or argue about things, but I've never known you to be very uptight and argumentative. What brought on this kind of attitude? The subject of Liam is sensitive and seems to upset you. Should I know something about it?"

"I'm sorry Zach, maybe you're right. Something's upsetting me, I'm not used to interrogation, it's as if I'm being accused of infidelity just because I'm getting friendly with Liam. Liam is a different kind of person that I've never encountered before, he's very easy-going, accommodating and jolly. I guess I'm used to your quiet, conservative and commanding demeanor. I've always looked up to you for guidance in all the things I've encountered in life, up until that time, you deserted me, which left me devastated. I would never be the grown woman that I am now with you. I would always be the little brat that needs your hand to guide me in life, that I would never be a woman with desires and sensuality like I felt when I was with Liam. He had not done anything except make me aware of his feelings for me, and how I responded to him."

"Why would you say that? Had you never wanted my kisses before, during those lonely moments? What did you feel when I touched you? I did not have to say a word but just looked at you, and you saw in my eyes how much I wanted you, then and now! I saw raw emotions in your eyes, afraid to keep on going for fear I would not be able to stop. I did not want to force you, it was not the right time. I want to take you now, come what may, but I see your hesitation, that's why I stopped and wondered what's holding you back. The only reason I could think of is Liam, which I'm right, you're comparing me to him!"

"Because you are the measure of the qualities I wanted in my soulmate! I wanted to feel the ecstasy I always get when I see you at the office or elsewhere! I'm still in awe, I've waited for this moment for a lifetime, and I'm truly overwhelmed and in a kind of trance, an enchanting gap between dream and reality."

"Is that true? Do you say this without a tinge of deceit to get me back to what I started early on before we got interrupted?" He looked at her with all the love he could convey and saw the glitter of joy in her eyes.

The way she looked at him melted the slightest doubt and jealousy in his heart, "Come here, give me what I long for, and make me feel the joy my soul has been searching for."

He took her lips for a tender kiss, her mouth opened to welcome and savor the taste of his tender love for her. Once more, the sensation took over them until they felt love's ecstasy. Long-held prisoner by time but true and lasting!

They were alone, all that mattered was that they were back to where they had always felt in their hearts. Zach, holding her tenderly, clinging to the tenderness of her soft body, enjoying the euphoric feelings engulfing them both. In the wee hours of the morning, Zach woke up and carefully carried Jasmine to her bed. After a while, he decided to lie next to her, embracing and caressing her softness whilst, smelling the scent that made him crazy. It reminded him of the early years when he would dance with her and cling to each other.

Tonight, he had advanced his privilege, lain next to her to touch and explore their sensuality. He was veiled with an aura of a predator, oozing virility tangible enough to cap every inch of her body. He savored and caressed her pliant body with his masculine energy, sensuality, and raw sexual expertise. His strong muscled thigh was only inches away from her glorious womanhood, his powerful shoulders dwarfing her, compelling her to surrender underneath him. Whatever was happening was meant to happen for the best reason possible! He was trying to salvage her love before it could be stolen away from him by Liam!

He caressed her thighs and felt her wetness. He felt the entrancing warmth of her womanhood, he listened to her soft moaning as he teased it. There were no signs of protest, his mouth covered hers, moving and probing in a breathtakingly insistent kiss. When his tongue slid inside her lips, his fingers found their way to caressing her and Jasmine lost the battle.

Jasmine desperately tried to hold on to her fleeting sanity, but when his tongue touched her tongue, her body arched against his sinewed muscled body and had lost her control. Every unconscious gesture seemed possessed by his rugged strength, alert sexual sophistication playing havoc inside her, and indomitable power over her. She felt unadulterated joy evoked by the prospect of being possessed by him completely. How could she let happiness elude her for a long time? Now, inhibition had no role in her well-being since Zach had complete, total control of her body. Zach gave her peace, her state of tranquility free from disquieting and oppressive thoughts of uncertainty and conflict. Without digging, she was able to unearth the truth of life, what makes her truly happy and complete.

It was always Zach! He was a river with still waters that ran deep! She was drowning in a sea of love filled with excitement and gratification that Zach had given her. What further insight could she ever be blessed with? It was by just letting Zach do what he wanted in their life together.

Her body, softness, and scent compelled his body to react, which stirred his hormones and heated his blood to perform the way he was making love to her. It whetted his appetite to be the best that walked the earth, giving her a world-shattering and passionate romantic ambiance. For the first time in her life, she felt desire with total wanton abandon, crazily wanting and taking whatever Zach was willingly giving her, enslaving her for a meager wink, creating havoc with a determination to keep things on an even keel.

He was just beginning, but his kiss was the kind that stoked a fire in her belly. It was playing footloose with her heart! He wanted her more than the air of life he breathed; he was lit ablaze with a desire that skittered across his spine in a rambunctious fashion. He felt as if he were possessed by the devil on his heels, raising hell!

Jasmine was breathless in wild anticipation and eagerness, with a passion that had lain dormant rising to the fore, drowning in a pounding swirl of blood and heat. Desire shot sharp through her, urging him to take her; her pulse skyrocketed. Her heart throbbed with demanding urgency and her breasts were splayed against his sinewy muscled chest. Raw lust filled his rigid erection that wanted to find the gate to heaven- the mating instinct, an elemental force between them that drove them to fever pitch passion. She moved her legs to allow and accommodate his powerful thighs against hers, rubbing insistently until she clutched his shirt as desperately for him as he was for her.

But Zach hesitated, an epiphany came to him. He had a morality check when he abruptly went down to her breasts and caressed them to his heart's content, guiding his hands along her soft curves, and abandoning his idea of taking her completely. He was not ready to take her virginity, he was guided and observant of his moral compass. It was alright to play and caress but not fully indulge until they were married. He did not stop his hot exploitation until they both got a climactic coming. The two were highly satisfied and slept peacefully afterward.

They both woke up at six in the morning, satisfied with themselves. They went to shower before heading to work with a promise of a repeat of their lovely night together, they agreed that Zach could visit and sleep over anytime he felt the need to make love to her.

However, Jasmine felt a bit awkward at the office. Each time she crossed paths with Zach, in the computer room or at the cafeteria, especially when approached by Zach with co-employees. He noticed their conflicting attitude of Jasmine, so he dropped by her office and locked the door behind him.

"What's wrong, my love? I feel that you're not comfortable talking with me around here. Did I do something that made you feel embarrassed or discomfited?"

"Not really, Zach. I'm just new to the feelings of familiarity and intimacy, and I'll get used to looking at you with that silly grin on your face. Sometimes when you tease me, I just want to hit you with a bat to vindicate myself."

"You can't do that to me here; I've nowhere to run and hide! I could put you across my lap and slap your bottom until you beg me to give you kisses instead!"

He was laughing and went to kiss her lightly on the lips and whispered, "I better watch myself carefully, else I'll get carried away and make love to you right here! Better tonight, be ready for me?" He then went to the door, gave her a wink and a wave, and left.

She went home much earlier than Zach; she needed to pick up some grocery items for easy cooking. She wanted to feel at ease and get rid of the anxiety of telling Liam about her and Zach. It was much easier to tell him that she got engaged to him, but that was not the case. She put away all the food items in the fridge and organized the canned goods in the pantry when the phone rang. She jumped anxiously to look at the caller ID, and it was Liam. She was thankful Zach was not there yet, else he could listen to their conversation.

"Hi, Liam, how's it going?" That was all she could say, afraid to stir doubts in him, knowing how perceptive he was.

"Good to hear your voice again. I was thinking of you and the memory of our dinner together fresh in my mind!"

He said appreciatively, with a smile in his voice that she could sense.

The moments when she danced close to Liam, it stirred sad emotions in Jasmine's heart. She could not speak casually, she felt choked by her feelings of loss, thinking she would never be able to recapture the magical spell. After a deep breath, she found the courage to spill the beans and tell him truthfully that she couldn't see him anymore and be friendly with him instead.

"Liam, I'm so sorry, but I need to tell you that I committed my heart to Zach last night. I'm sure you'll not want any furtherance of our acquaintance, at least, the way we were that night, dancing." She felt the heaviness of her request and knew that it was disheartening to him as it was to her.

"What happened? Why, in such a short time, you decided my fate? Did I not deserve a bit of a chance to prove the worth of my acquaintance?" He asked, evidently surprised at her abrupt decision to choose Zach over him. Actually, when they met a week ago, he had been given a chance, but their chemistry was great! They responded positively to each other in a romantic, sensual way.

"Please, don't feel bad, it's that Zach and I have a decade of history between us. He was everything to me when I was growing up. It devastated me when he left, but he came back looking for me, and we were already on the verge of commitment when I met you. Yes, you and I have a lot in common, but it is not opportune for us to grow emotionally because I have no right to love again. I can't hold you back, it's not fair. Perhaps, had we met when I had retreated from love, I could have regained my trust in love and be with you."

"I don't blame you for my misfortune, I've learned a lot about your relationship with Zach from Sue and Julie, but I took the chance to be near you to satisfy my curiosity. Zach is lucky indeed for the second chance you gave him, I hope he lives to enjoy and cherish you in his life."

"I just want you to know that I consider myself lucky for having met and felt your closeness, even only for a moment in time! Had I not taken a second chance at Zach's heart, I would have found a new love in you! I'm sorry, it is not our time!"

"Thank you, Jasmine, I will cherish that in my heart. I wish you all the happiness in this world and when I see you again, I know that I have a special place in your heart. I truly appreciate your courage and conviction. You take care, good bye."

"God bless you, Liam. I wish you the best in life, true love will find and come your way sooner than you may wish for. Thank you for the joy you've given me during the short time I've known you. Goodnight and goodbye." She hung up the phone and was so sad that tears fell from her eyes. She would miss Liam, a lot, in her life. She felt sorrow gripping her heart, she had a special reverence for him!

When Zach called, she was already in bed, "How's my lady love, still feeling uneasy about us getting intimate and lovey-dovey?"

His voice was really in that teasing mood, "I'm here dreaming of the ecstasy you gave me last night and wishing I'm next to you, holding you close and tight."

"Stop teasing me and wipe that silly grin on your face," She said but did not sound defensive or bothered, "I love you, Zach and I feel the comfort and security of your arms around me. I'm just not used to being touched and kissed the way you do, we never did those things before."

"Well, sweetie, get used to it and a lot more you don't know, but I hope I don't scare you away! Love works in mysterious ways and we learn more as we grow together. Loving is living, and living is loving! How was grocery shopping, nobody accosted my most delectable beloved? I worry so much about you, men are drawn to you, fascinated and awed."

"Nothing like that. All is well, and thanks for the morale boost!"

"Do you have anything to tell me?" He said as his intuition was well-tuned to her.

She needed to be truthful, even though she was still very emotional with Liam's disappointment in his pursuit of her, "Liam called."

"And what happened? Did you honestly tell him about us?" Zach exclaimed.

"Of course, I did. I wanted him to know where we stood so that he would be spared of the heartache. I would never dream of leading him on when I could not give him what he wanted in a relationship." She sounded so sad. It touched

Zach's heart, but he told her it was fitting and proper to be direct no matter how the truth may hurt.

"He'll accept his fate quietly. He has not invested any of his time with you. I feel his pain, though. It's not often that one could meet someone like you who possesses all the qualities of a desirable wholesomeness of womanhood! He'll be thankful in the long run and would appreciate your decision to halt any more interactions between you. Did you cancel your dinner date for next week?"

"There was no need, we said our goodbyes. We decided to be just friendly and casual if we crossed paths again. We are all friends, and there is no need to alienate anyone."

"Thank you, love. That is one less worry for you and me. I appreciate your promptness in addressing that issue. You'll find it would be a lot better for you, I know you are fond of him, and the least you wanted was to hurt and disappoint him. I like him, too. I thought he liked Julie when they spent time after the party. I think Liam is trustworthy, I would not mind if he went after Julie, but not you." He made it clear, he did not want Liam anywhere around her.

That made her think about Julie. Could Liam possibly fall in love with her? If he wanted to get involved with Julie, the two did not have a lot in common. In comparasion, Jasmine and Julie were at the opposite end of the spectrum, though both were appealing and attractive. Jasmine was mature and experienced, while Julie was young and had no known relationship. Jasmine was educated and professional, Julie was still in school. Jasmine was a bit conservative and Julie was liberal and daring, but on the other hand, both were femme fatale, and men were fascinated by them! And both had similar taste, respect, admiration, and fascination for Liam's virile personality!

Would she feel unaffected if Liam switched his attention and affection to Julie? Would she feel slightly jealous, maybe? That had to be seen in the future if Liam and Julie's relationship materialized. They had already met, and Julie was surely able to hold his attention for the rest of the night.

Over the weekend, Jasmine asked Suzy to come and have an impromptu visit with her to talk about girly things. She came over and enjoyed the afternoon in her garden, she also had a lot of thoughts to unload!

"Nice to see you again, girl, what a lovely afternoon it is! Hmmm, what's that smelling good food?"

Jasmine knew that Suzy loved her pan-fried pork barbecue and cold lemonade. She also made cold shrimp salad with minced crunchy veggies, topping it with a dessert of cheesecake and black cherry ice cream.

"Are we pigging out the whole afternoon? You're on, let's forget the calories!"

"Yeah, why not? It's a good thing to do, breathe in and exhale once in a while!" She led her to her favorite spot in the backyard, shaded and very private amidst the fragrant late blooms of the summer. "Take the best seat in the garden, relax, and just spend the day away while listening to music."

"You did not ask me to come here and vegetate, right? You have a lot in your mind, a lot going on in your life, and you have no idea how to deal and go about life without making a mess and being sorry later?" Suzy said, knowing how Jasmine was, especially when confronted with heart problems.

"Well, you know me better than I know myself. I'm perplexed and deeply confused about how to deal with Zach, this time overwhelmed with his attention, and I feel suffocated and need a breather. Also, I'm bothered by Liam, I felt I've not given him enough space and justice with what I've thrown in his midst."

"What did you do this time? You mesmerized him with your beguiling beauty, awed him with your intellectual prowess, and now cast Liam, Mr. Perfect, in an abyss of frustration? And you're lovey-dovey with Zach, the unconventional Mr. Right?"

She felt her exasperation and was herself, unsure how to untangle the mess, "You better start from the beginning and not overlook anything, so we can fully work this mess out! First, give me a piece of that sweet, spicy tasting meat whetting my appetite!"

"Well, you know how Liam is, you're right to call him Mr. Perfect, his stature and demeanor, his almost perfect looks, his loving manners, but most of all his sexual prowess. Not that he awed me with that, but he cast a magic spell on me by just being himself, slow dancing with me, in complete magical silence, which made me aware of how magnetic and bewildering his virility was. It engulfed my being and I became helpless to his oozing charm."

As Jasmine spoke of Liam, Suzy knew what she was talking about, the magical aura that veiled her when in the presence of Liam's persona. He was truly a masculine and attractive person. Still, his quiet ways, of looking through your eyes, and slow-moving gestures were very calculating and subtle. Yet forceful when his sensuality played a very enticing role in captivating your heart and affection, hold you in full attention to his charm.

"To tell you the truth, every woman who was fortunate enough to meet and get acquainted with Liam shared the same concept of him. He's as natural and awesome as the fresh air you breathe early in the morning, after the rain, and in the early evening under the moon and the stars! He can make any woman fall in love with him, but too bad for him, you're the first woman who denied him the chance to know you better. Worst for you for having missed the greatest fascination of your love life!" Suzy said in defense of Liam.

She looked at Jasmine, who was quietly listening as she continued on, "I could have asked for just a little bit of it if he had let me any closer. To me, he was very elusive, he would not even want to look at me straight so that I could gaze directly into those intense blue eyes! You don't know how intriguing it was to contemplate the joy of knowing him, let alone be held close to his heart! I was madly awed by him, but to him, I was the dull little sister of his friend and did not merit his time. Just maybe, he could have spared me a scrap of attention if I dropped my cone of ice cream."

"In short, I am crazy for letting Liam go and choosing Zach; the old hat, the cool, conservative, and distant lover I considered the master of my heart?" Jasmine, looking gravely and anticipating Suzy's response.

"If I would make a wish right now, nothing else, except to grace the honor of Liam's attention! I would bet my last dollar on him! I've always been fascinated by his personality, a believer in the magnitude of his trustworthy character and a fan of his playful manners. Quite endearing to all the people whose lives he had touched so far!" Suzy showed her true understanding of Liam, and Jasmine felt her friend held deep admiration and possibly nurtured an unrequited love for Liam.

"You have known Liam for a long while, why did the two of you never develop a relationship other than close friendship? You seemed to be truly in awe of him and his qualities. You have not been going out with anybody, and you never even mention anyone in our conversation. No one special to you even exists, but with Liam as the topic, you're all attention and full of interest, and your eyes light up. You are in love with Liam, aren't you, my friend?"

"You've caught me red-handed as a fish caught in the mouth! Yes, but Liam is very principled. He probably thinks being in business with my brother, he's also my keeper and will not be caught in any way compromising, having an eye on me, the younger sister of his associate!"

She exhaled with frustration but was resigned to accept it, not to upset the business balance between him and her brother, "His friendship is very important to me. At least, I have something with him! I'm very attentive to his needs when he's staying with us. I wish he would stay in the house with me, it's scary being alone!"

"Don't you think Jasper would rather have you get involved with someone he knows and respects than with any devil he does not know? Why not test the water to find out for yourself, talk to Jasper about it, possibly even tell him the truth that you consider Liam a good candidate for your affection, that he is respectable and trustworthy!"

"I don't know if I can do that. Like you, I have my pride, we are never aggressive and open-minded as the millennials are. I normally wait to be asked, not to assume anything, especially in dealing with the opposite sex. I don't want to shock Liam and be shunned for being forward and stealing a man's thunder and his privilege to take his pick! But years back, Jasper teased me about having a crush on him since I was twelve years old. Liam knew about it but never felt arrogant like it was nothing!"

"Well, there are other ways, you know. But I don't like your idea of make-believe regarding your interest in Joven than with Liam. Next time he visits, have a nice talk with him, ask him questions of his interest, be casual and friendly. Unload that nice smile of yours, be engaging by looking into his eyes and be interesting! He probably will find it easier because you're the one offering the chance to know him better, that way, he's not guilty of seducing the little sister of his business partner."

Jasmine, looking at her, felt that Suzy was clearly picking up on the strategy to catch the attention of Liam rather than hide and wait for him to seek her company, especially when in LA to stay at her place. She should be entertaining him and seeking his advice.

"Okay, thanks for the pep talk about how I'll manage to steal Liam's attention from you. Let's discuss what's overwhelming about your relationship with Zach. But before we do that, I'm starved! Let me try this shrimp salad you made. Looks yummy, and I know how you love seafood, I do, too! This salad is good in really complementing the taste of the barbecued pork, being pan-fried, I should learn how to make them, maybe dazzle Liam next time he comes!"

"You should, that will be a good excuse to get to know him better. Later, when you're all alone with your brother, ask him a lot about Liam, that way, you could make him aware of your interest in him without outright confessing."

"Actually, Jasper wanted Liam to stay at home a long time ago, but I refused the idea then, I wanted privacy. I did not want him around and saw how I was conscious of him. But now I'll do that, I'm already excited! Do you think Liam could be interested in me, right after being besotted with you? I know I can't hold a candle to your spectacular personality, you've got that 'it' guys are crazy about."

"Don't say that, beauty is subjective! Opposite attracts! Let him fall in love with you, being you and not emulating other women. Be yourself, being open and honest would endear you to him, I know that because I came closer to his heart!"

"Okay, now tell me about Zach, what happened between the two of you? Other than the things you have already told me and complained about."

Suzy now confronted Jasmine about the overwhelming incident that made her discontinue her budding friendship with Liam, who showed amorous interest in her.

"He learned about my dinner date with Liam and he called me to his office when I was done for the day and about to go home. He was furious and his attitude was accusatory, which did not go well with me, so I bit back. He followed me home and said to resolve all the issues that were messing both our lives."

"How did he learn about the dinner date? You're not the 'kiss and tell' kind of a girl, especially after a nice date with someone you're trying to hide from his jealous rage?" Suzy contemplated who the culprit was who could have divulged the details of the secret date.

"It's not important, but I have a hunch, and he was not bluffing. He described the slow dancing and the moment's intimacy with remarkable detail. He was really jealous and afraid I was falling in love with Liam and he became a threat to him or our so-called 'love affair.' He brought finger food, so I would not 'waste' my time feeding us and promptly took the matters into his hand. He was in total control, and I was the fly on the wall, with no guts to say no to what he imposed on me, what he planned for us!"

She sat looking away from Suzy, avoiding a direct confrontation of her true feelings for Zach. Suzy knew she was confusing love with the attention and sensuality of Liam in front of her, taking precedence over her dismay with Zach for not asserting his love over her. She had waited long for Zach to claim his rights over her heart, body, and soul. She could no longer presume that his love was hers and not Julie's. She was ready to turn to Liam!

"After dinner, he sat there comfortably and tried to seduce me with his short talk, but it did not move the needle. At those moments, the memory of the sensuality I experienced with Liam unconsciously held me back from reacting to Zach's bidding. I was cold and distant and wanted nothing between us, that left me confused and doubtful about our state of affairs."

Jasmine was quiet before continuing her story, "He took me with him, seated close to each other on the couch at the den, and he started kissing me. His play was subtle and getting passionate and long, but I was still in a state of shock and was still entranced by Liam's virile power over me. We fell asleep on the couch, when he woke up, he carried me to the bed and lay next to me. He held me close and started caressing me, without any sign of protest from me, so he continued. He whispered that he had realized we had a life to live, a love to share. Subsequently, we would continue to do what he wanted us to share until we're ready to get married. At the time Julie would have graduated and out of our lives."

"You mean you went all the way? What if you got pregnant?" Suzy asked solicitously and in great suspense and worried for her.

"No, he stopped, and we did not go all the way because he said he owed that to me. He'd gladly take me completely when we're already married, only we'll indulge in acts allowed to lovers and not be afraid to express our love in any way we find acceptable and pleasurable to both of us at our convenience. We'll be discreet, and he will sleep over to my place every so often we desire to make love."

"That's the way you want it, right? To feel his love, have his attention on you instead of on Julie. So, what's eating you up? If I'm in your position, I'll be singing his praise! You got what you wished for!" Suzy teased whilst smiling happily.

"I don't truly know how I feel. What's still missing in my life, you're right, I've waited for that moment to come when he would kiss me passionately and touch me the way he never did before. Now, I'm confused. I don't know what I want, Liam is always on my mind, I don't want to know what I might have lost by shutting him out of my life. But it's done now. I'm left to sort out what is left, Zach and me!"

"Tell me, you love Zach all the way. Aren't you happy? He finally realized how important you're in his love life? And he's got plans on how the two of you can enjoy life while waiting for Julie to be independent and out of his responsibility. What could be better than that? And hey, you will feel a lot in control when he puts that engagement ring on your finger!" Suzy said that with utmost confidence.

"I hope that's the missing link to all of my thoughts coming together! But, thank you, I feel better having told you all my worries. We'll be better off knowing we have an alternative solution to whatever comes before us, that hope is always there if we have faith in our hearts!" Jasmine thought she wanted a commitment now.

They finished the food, then relaxed and promised to keep each other posted on everything happening between them. Suzy expressed hope that Liam would spend more time here in Los Angeles and stay with her instead of in different hotels, which would give her security and the chance to know him. That gave a little satisfaction to Jasmine, knowing that his short-lived fascination could just be a short infatuation and could be overcome by Suzy's plan, he needed to find his true North.

She woke up early that Sunday morning, planned to go to church, then do some window shopping and possibly a light lunch in one of her favorite restaurants nearby the beach. She had just walked out of the shower when the phone rang.

"Hello, Zach, good morning! Are you up, I thought you would be sleeping in?"

"How's my favorite belle? I thought of you all day. Yesterday I was fighting the urge to come to your door, but didn't. Now, I have to see you."

"What are you planning?" She said but did not tell him about her plans already set for the day.

"A solemn Sunday morning to attend church with me, walk to the beach, light lunch in one of your favorite restaurants by the coast, do some window shopping. Finish the day, possibly, the night with you?"

"I think I have telepathically transmitted that to you but only up to window shopping!"

"That's true, but what is more exciting and more gratifying is spending more time with you! Quality time for us to share, more than anything. Shall I pick you up around 9:30? Let's attend the mass that starts at 10 am? Okay?" Happily, both hung up.

At exactly the given time, Zach was at the curb in front of her house. She walked out and went straight to him, locking the gate behind her. She gave him a beautiful smile as he opened the car door for her, driving away to where they would attend church.

Later, they went around the stores scattered along the coastline, and exactly at noon, they went to eat lunch. After a sumptuous lunch, Zach asked the waiter to clear their table and bring them their ordered dessert.

"Take your sweet time to savor the cheesecake, I like watching you enjoy your cake!" He was in a very light, happy mood, watching her brimming with lovely energy.

Zach motioned the waiter to come to their table, then he took out a small red box, knelt before Jasmine, and said emphatically, "Jasmine Jade Warloffe, will you marry me and give me the honor to be my wife?"

"Yes, Zach, I will marry you and be your wife. I love you!" She extended her hand, and Zach slipped the diamond engagement ring on her finger.

The waiter took many pictures as they kissed, sealing their engagement through happy poses and shining smiles. The two savored the missing happiness since they reunited after years of separation. The uncertainty became the wedge in their relationship, but now Zach sealed their love by asking her hand in marriage. Jasmine felt renewed and certain that never again would they be apart, and it made her aware that it was what she had waited for in a long time, Zach's commitment to love her for all eternity!

Jasmine felt ecstatic and was walking on clouds, anticipating another sweet moment with Zach, knowing he was hers and no one could take him away from her, not even

Julie! Finally, she was not his second, but his first and only love! She had lots of pictures to prove it and for posterity to show that Zach's love found its way to her and that her love for Zach was fully requited! Her lonely days were over, and she was looking forward to more rewarding moments with him

It was past three o'clock in the afternoon when they reached Jasmine's place. Zach carried her across the threshold, and when he put her down, he kissed her most tenderly and said, "Today and forward, I'll love and honor you for the rest of our days!" She kissed back Zach and repeated the same promise.

He took out a can of beer and ginger ale to raise a toast to Jasmine, "To us!" And then he went to the computer and happily sent an email to friends announcing their engagement.

Later, he called Julie, who was delighted that her beloved brother and Jasmine finally made the best decision in their lives, sealing their love for each other.

Liam heard the news from Suzy when she called Jasper in San Francisco, where he was staying and working on their latest contract.

"Hey bro, may I talk to Liam if he's right there with you?" Bravely, Suzy asked to talk to Liam, staying with Jasper for a few days.

They were expecting it, but it was better to know that the engagement had finally happened. To Liam, on the subject of his growing fondness of Jasmine, it was definite that love eluded him this time. He thought of his love for Susy, long unspoken, whom he had grown to like dearly, and care about but had refrained from getting involved because of his prevailing partnership with her brother. His closeness to the family was complicated. He wanted to find the comfort and joy of courting his prospective love for Suzy, so near yet so far!

A bit surprised but elated, Jasper said, "Sure, sis, why do you suddenly want to talk to my old friend here? Are you getting lonely or desperate to grow old without a guy in your life? You're not a spinster yet, Sue!" He turned to Liam and said with gladness, "Here, Liam, one desperate spinster wants your attention!" He screamed in the back while handing the phone to Liam.

"Hey you, what's up? I heard about the news. Today's their day to celebrate, we'll have our time pretty soon, don't you think so?"

Encouraged by that, she countered joyfully, breaking the ice with Liam, "Yeah, we'll have ours, sooner than we could ever wish for! It's getting lonely, and I'm envious. Some of our friends got married while others are engaged and we're still single!"

"Don't worry, I'll be home by Friday evening, pick me up at the airport at about 7 pm and I'll take you out dining and dancing, and we'll celebrate a new beginning, how's that?" He said, making sure Jasper was listening, and he winked at him, making sure he was reading his reaction loud and clear! Jasper smiled and gave him a thumbs-up.

"Are you kidding me? That's the best offer I got and for sure I won't miss it for a million bucks. Just kidding, don't scurry away, I don't bite! See you then, thanks!" Suzy hung up and felt some kind of happiness she could not decipher, something she wished for when the subject of Liam came to mind these days!

After talking to Liam, Suzy called Jasmine and told her the good news, "My wish is coming to realization, and thanks for the advice, it's working! Liam is treating me to dinner and told me he'll be staying with me that night. I told him that he could stay with me instead of sleeping at his office or hotel for security reasons. It's getting dangerous for me to be living alone."

"That's the best practical idea coming from you, and it will serve a double purpose. Not only giving you peace of mind for security and a way to know Liam better. The two of you are a good match, and living together will give you two a chance to know each other. I'm sure your brother will be the happiest, he can stop worrying about your safety, and he doesn't have to come to LA twice a month just to check on you!"

"I'll keep my fingers crossed, hoping the best is yet to come!" Suzy said with hope and joy evident in her voice, "I'll let you go, but I'll give you an update! I'm so excited to see Liam, thanks to you. Bye!"

After the call from Suzy was over, Jasmine sat there thinking about Liam, his kindness and his very affable ways, his warm and easy-going style, truly endearing. Suzy was lucky to be living with him, she felt a bit envious!

Zach and Jasmine were contemplating their newfound happiness, sitting comfortably at the wide couch where Zach started making Jasmine aware of his desires to be intimate with her a few nights before. He looked at her with that tenderness in his blue eyes, kissing her sweetly. He found her lips parted, waiting for him to explore her long and unsated desire.

She sought his most immediate passion for taking her to the peak of ecstasy. She encouraged him to explore the warmth of her mouth, opening up to where passion sought ecstasy. He reclined, taking her down with him without breaking the hot kiss. With strength of purpose, his hands started caressing her body, one hand cupping the fullness of her breast. Jasmine responded by inching closer to him, clinging in a tightened embrace, desperately seeking gratification from her awakened sensuality. They were riding the waves of raptured ecstatic intimacy, alien to their souls. Gradually, their impassioned emotions welcomed them into a new world of joy and pleasure. Jasmine's restlessness about intimacy before engagement and marriage was thrown out of the equation, she was now a willing participant in his dance to attain the utmost pleasure a loving couple could possibly attain.

Just as Zach and Jasmine were ushering themselves to a higher level of intimacy, Suzy was starting to consider the possibility of awakening Liam's feelings towards her. She knew how nice and accommodating Liam was to her before. She learned of his measured standard scruples, that of respecting a sibling of an associate, not for him to exploit her, that the excuse of falling in love with her was not allowed in deference to his relationship with her brother.

In that regard, Suzy was not sure whether Liam or she was mistaken in reading Jasper's concern. Looking back, it was Jasper who was encouraging Suzy to convince Liam to stay at their LA home with her during business trips. She knew she was the one who declined the idea, afraid that it could alienate anyone interested in her, that it was her reputation at stake that could be compromised by having a male friend living with her.

Although Jasper thought the idea was good for her safety and protection, he gave in to her wishes. But he gave a room in the house exclusively for Liam's use for all his things and his expensive car, a Porsche, had a spot in their garage. He stayed at the home whenever he could to check on Suzy every once in a while. Suzy admired his Porsche, the German Volkswagen group made it. They also created the small but inexpensive car known as the efficient beetle!

Friday evening, Suzy was dressed in a casual jumper made of denim over her peach-colored blouse, very dainty and becoming on her slim stature showing her long shapely legs and subtle feminine curves. She was not a voluptuous young woman, per se, but the fullness of her bosom was evident that gave her an edge to attract attention to sensuality. Liam's delight was showing in his attractive smile, and his sex appeal was intoxicating to Suzy, who felt her cheeks warmed at his sight. She hurried her steps towards him, and Liam gave her a bear hug and a very tender squeeze of her slim shoulder.

"Welcome back, Liam!"

"So nice to see you, it seemed longer since that birthday bash you had!" He put his hand on her shoulder and led her away, "Where did you park your best buddy?"

"Oh, my best buddy, the parking lot was full, it's just across the street. I got lucky when I drove in, a car just pulled out of the curb." She said, pointing to her beloved little but very efficient yellow-green volks.

"You love that car, and it's good for you. Dependable and just the right size to park anywhere in the city." He said, appreciating the car and her penchant for it.

"Yeah, I can call it Porsche's little sister! Who would not appreciate her? She's reliable, never misses or hard on me and my reckless speeding!" She said smilingly to him.

"That's what I want you to stop doing; speeding never pays. It will only give you trouble, good if it's just a nasty wreck but what about yourself? I would not have you waste your life trying to gain a few-minute travel time. You know what I mean?" He stopped and looked at her seriously, "You matter to me. I want you to keep that in your pretty little head, I'm not kidding!"

She gave her a silly grin, then said, "Okay, Liam, I hear you! Thanks for caring!"

"It's no joke, Sue. From now on, I'm responsible for your safety! I've ignored Jasper before, but now I realize that's what I should be preoccupied with!" He waited for Suzy to unlock the passenger door; he shoved his traveling bag inside and sat on the passenger side, next to her. "Do you know that swanky little place near the beach? That's where I want to take you tonight!"

"That's too expensive, stylish and formal. Why can't we just go to Wendy's for fries and hamburgers, let's reserve the stylish place for a special occasion, okay?"

She tapped his hand, holding her hand break, "Release the brake, I'm the driver, and I will go to where I want to take you. You're my guest, after dinner, I'll take you home with me, no buts!" She said brazenly, nodded to him and drove away much to his surprise.

"Am I seeing a different you? An attractive young woman with determination and strong will?" He said, looking at her affectionately, "I've just been gone over a week, and here you are, well-transformed into a mature and sophisticated woman. Did that one year change you?" Keeping his humor, he added, "I kind of like it, entertaining, engaging and encouraging! Carry on, my dear, I'm delighted!"

"Liam, Liam, you don't know anything about me. Over the ten years you've been coming and going in my life, never did you stop to ponder who I am! Of course, not aged like sweet wine, but just grown up now! To you, I am always the little brat sister of your friend. Good for naughty pranks with giggly belligerent stanches. Well, be surprised, I'm more than that and you'll never know who you are dealing with now!"

"Oh, yeah? Amazing! Could you show me the new you? I'm obliged to meet the matured woman who aged like sweetened, expensive wine! I'm in for a rude awakening!"

Looking at her with more scrutiny trying to check on the transformational changes that happened in his short absence.

They came to her chosen trendy fast-food place, and she parked the car like a breeze! She looked at him and said, "Come, and we'll settle a lot of scores here!"

She smiled and looked at him beguilingly. She made that stance to Liam's delight, making him smile with anticipation. With the enchantment and pure joy, Suzy made his day enjoyable with plenty of surprises.

"Get us a cozy corner, please, while I order our food." He said to her.

He went to the counter and made the order, after taking his number, he went to the men's room to wash his hands. Suzy waved at him when he reappeared. He picked up their order and sat, "Good, this is quieter here, not too busy tonight. Do I start asking questions, or you'll dazzle me with all the changes in your personality, demeanor, and taste over things?"

"Well, I can tell you some, like in my taste or preference, in food, in looks, in company of other people, but with other things, you just have to observe if there are any differences from before to the after."

"Number one, you sound intriguing and interesting! Is Joven aware of this neat transformation?" Liam, still looking fascinated, was interestingly engaging her.

"What has Joven got to do with me?" She asked, surprise evident in her voice.

"Isn't he your boyfriend? Of course, he's the first one to be affected by the changes in your attitude. Jasper and I are only secondary. Joven is the primary person concerned." He queried, unsure whether she was not happy he mentioned Joven.

"For your information, Joven is not my boyfriend, never was and never will be! He is a friend of a close friend who hangs around us." She said with emphasis, looking at him intently, making her statement come across loud and clear!

"Okay, so that is clear to me now, and I promise never to implicate your name with him. If I may ask, is there someone who's in your love sphere at this very moment in time?"

"Why do you ask? Are you interested?" She said, instantaneously without processing the thought, outrageously unforgiven, but it was too late. It was out already. She looked at the shock that slightly registered on Liam's face. "Sorry, I was too fast and offensive. I didn't mean it that way. I misspoke!"

"If I may advise, calm down, say it slowly but surely. Your hormones are reaping havoc on your young mind. You think you know things, but in reality, you're just halfway through the baby steps to attain maturity. Don't worry about me; I understand you fully well! No offense intended by you, so none taken." Liam noticed it bothered her, and she had lost her enthusiasm. "Sue, I have always been your staunch supporter and admirer- nothing you can say or do will change the way I look at you. My perception and feelings will stay the same!"

"Thank you, Liam. I don't want to lose that- I'll hang on to it to make me strong and be worth your friendship." Liam reached for her hands and squeezed them in his, and he felt some strange thing in himself as he stared at her. She looked down, then, with an embarrassed gaze, looked up at Liam. He, for the first time, had noticed how expressive her hazel eyes were, slightly hidden underneath in the mascara she had painted on her eyelids covering the lush lashes, her nose was very proportional to her face, and her lips were in an attractive pout that was sensual to look at, she typified a young woman with a growing sensuality in the way she looked, talked, moved.

Liam, becoming aware of her budding sensuality, could not help but say, "Remember, I'm always at your beck and call. I want you to know that I'll never be too busy or far away if you need me. Any time I consider it a privilege to be at your side whenever you want me, I'll be there for you! Is that clear?"

"Yes, Liam, I hope I did not disappoint you by being anxious to show you that I'm now a grown woman worthy of attention. Please don't treat me like the little brat that I was before. I know I did some crazy things before."

"Not to me. I was there amused by your courageous stunts! Some are very funny, and others may be described as vicious like when you chased the neighbor boys with a bat!" He smiled charmingly at her and watched her blush a little bit. He knew she had a crush on him as she admitted brazenly, without hesitation, when she was confronted by her brother one silly afternoon about why she was hanging around, always pestering them. They all laughed out loud, and that was never mentioned.

She went back to her thoughts, "I told you, I have some things to talk to you about." This time she appeared serious and not in a joking mood.

"Go ahead. I'm listening." Liam said, taking her seriously this time, dimmed the silly mischievous gleam in his blue eyes, listened, and concentrated on Suzy's beautiful face and her sultry lips.

"Don't dislike me for this, but I fought hard with Jasper when I chucked his proposal that you live with me in the house here in LA as you were living with him whenever you're in San Francisco. I was crazy. I wanted to live alone- no friend or stranger with me in the house. I'm sorry for that now." She looked at Liam gravely, assessing his reaction to what she had just said.

"I know that, and I understood your position and never faulted or criticized you for it; it was your prerogative." He explained to her that he was not offended at all, nor had taken that against her.

"What would you say if I reversed my decision? I want you to stay with me whenever you're here in LA." She looked at him earnestly, trying to read his reaction, whether there was surprise or hesitance.

"Why the change of heart? Not on account of Jasper, I suppose." He said without any hint of doubt but for want of certainty, clarity of her purpose.

"No, not on account of Jasper, but at my own volition. Truthfully, I'm getting more aware of the times we're living in now, scared of home invasions that are prevalent in the city. With you around, whenever would give me peace of mind. I recently noticed suspicious cars with drivers reading newspapers and watching houses around, about people coming and going. I did not tell Jasper, afraid of alarming him, else he'll be coming over here every weekend. Or persistently bugging you to check and drive by every day. That would be a nuisance. Would you care to consider my proposition? I feel safer knowing you're around!"

"Are you proposing for us to live together?"

"Silly you! Not in that compromising way! I can't hold a candle to Jasmine. I'm not competing- I know you like her a lot, but too bad, her heart has been taken by Zach a long,

long time ago! I'm only here to seek your company and friendship, not to force you to take me." She looked sad, torn between thoughts. Was it because Liam was more interested in Jasmine than he could ever be with her, or that Liam wanted his privacy more than taking the responsibility to protect her?

"What about you? I know that you're concerned about your reputation and privacy. It might be more compromising for you than for me to be living together without any blood connection. We're only friends, and some people would view that as something indiscreet and irreputable!"

"It's my life, and I couldn't care less what people would think. I know you're a person with integrity and respectability. The question is would you care to be with me, day in and day out, while you're not in a relationship with any woman of your choice? I can understand that, and I'll be the first to set you free whenever you find her and want to be with her in your life. In the meantime, I beg you to reconsider my proposition!"

"How do you propose to live?" He asked if there were rules to follow.

"No rules, except our inherent decency and sense of responsibility. I will treat you with the highest respect and utmost regard, be accommodating and considerate, cooperative, nice, and friendly in every way! I'll even cook for you and wash your laundry while you're designing houses. I swear on my parent's grave!"

Agreeing to move with her, he said, "That's even better than the pledge of allegiance I used to recite in school! Where's the part that says 'to have and to hold, to love and to cherish?' Come here." He slid closer to her side of the upholstered semi-round seat and put his arms around her. "You need not promise all that. I know how good you are and will take good care of me as you do of Jasper. You're young, but your responsibility and character speak volumes. You're advanced and way up the measures of maturity."

"That means you'll accept and live with me?" She wanted an explicit verbal commitment from Liam.

"Yes, Sue, from now on, you're the Good Witch in my life with your magic wand to order me around, to be at your beck and call! Wait until I call Jasper to tell him about our new arrangement- he'll be thrilled beyond measure. I'll take care of all the bills, food and grocery, and whatever is needed to continue the maintenance and steady upkeep of the house with us living together." Liam wished, *"Until death do us part!"*

They sealed their agreement with a tight embrace and a kiss on her forehead. She was very appreciative and told Liam he made her the happiest woman on earth!

Liam said, "I thought a woman is the happiest on earth when she's married to her beloved husband!"

To which he got an answer from Suzy, "It would be, whatever, whenever!"

Part #4

Zach and Jasmine were watching the news, spending quality time after their engagement. Zach was tenderly stroking her arms and looking at her with his intense and prying eyes, "How are you feeling, engaged to me, has anything changed in your perspective?" He waited for her, who looked up at him, thinking what best would she say to calm his inquisitive mind.

"Zach darling, of course, I'm ecstatic and delighted that at last, you found a way to reconcile with your restless dreams, a way to resolve all important issues confronting your conscience and reality! For myself, it has given me peace and cleared every gnawing doubt in my mind, whether you truly love me or am I just playing second fiddle to your heart. It has eliminated the wedge between us, thus making me more demonstrative of my feelings for you. Nothing is holding me back now, knowing you are with me all the way!"

"I knew it was the right time to ask you, to propose marriage- that way, we both could move on to more important things in our lives. Having weaned ourselves from the obstacles that hindered us, especially you, it set you free to look at things in a different light."

"I'm happy for us. Now we can start planning our lives. Where would you like to live, here or at your place, of course, after the wedding?"

"I'm not waiting for our wedding- I'm moving in with you here, right away. I can't live without you next to me, like now. I like holding you in my arms. I'll check my household once in a while, and Julie can have our housekeeper stay with her."

"Zach, you sound facetious! Your state of carnal bliss is clouding your mind, overwhelmed with the novelty of your emotions. After you're used to having me around, your appetite for lovemaking would dissipate or waft away."

"You don't have the slightest idea of how a man in love feels, do you? You don't know how hard I tried to quash my appetite to make love when near you, and when away, eager and wanting to be near and lose myself in your softness!"

And right that moment, his lips came down to claim her mouth, his tongue eager to explore the warmth that made him crazy and propelled his appetite to fever pitch once more. Without much kissing foreplay, his hand began caressing her body down to her thighs, searched the wetness of her womanhood, and unapologetically entered her slick inner sanctum, whose utmost privacy and inviolability were sacred, but the wetness and warmth almost drove him crazy whetting his desire to take her. They were both helpless; only their uneven breaths laboring hard spoke of the hot passion scorching their bodies with an overwhelming force that had engulfed them completely. This was the scenario the two of them were playing, engaging when overwhelmed with passion. They lost themselves enthralled with ecstasy in the heat of passion!

Jasmine was happy she had her life to live and all her love to give Zach, after surviving the loneliness of nights waiting if love would really touch her life again! And it had!

Suzy was glad Liam agreed to her proposition. She would find the right time to tell Jasper of the good news. She was sure Jasper would be delighted with her plans- there was no need to worry about her and her safety because Liam would be there to look after her and the household!

The garage opened as they came to the driveway, and the car lights shone on Liam's Porsche parked inside. Liam said, "My Porsche is sure glad to see me! I'd like to drive you around the coast one evening when you're home early. How's that?"

"That would be nice! You're on. Nothing I'd like better than driving along the area one moonlit night, enjoying the breeze, and being dazzled by a multitude of stars!" Suzy gladly accepted his invitation, thinking what could be better than that! He was coming along nicely to her, as she had wished.

Inside the house, Suzy laid more plans for Liam. "How would you like to take the bigger room so that you have a place to work on your drawings. It's not being used, only to house junk that should be thrown away. That way, you could have all your things together instead of here and there." She looked at him to see if her plan or suggestion was acceptable to him. "Come on! I'll set it up for you- I'm a practical decorator!"

"Are you sure? What about Jasper? He might need it more when he's here in LA?" Liam was apprehensive but thought the idea was very good for him.

"No, in fact, he told me to offer it to you then, and now that you're here, he'll want the same. Go for it! I'll help organize your stuff, I know you have other drawings in the garage, and you can use that long sturdy table and the swivel chair. There is an empty drawer in the other room, you can use that to store other things. We just have to look and find other things like lampshades and other electrical gadgets that would be useful. Trust me!"

"Thank you. You're an angel! Let's take it easy and do that tomorrow, and for sure, I want and need your help." Liam approached her and touched her by the shoulder, saying, "What good luck has come my way- you are wonderful!"

Looking satisfied with all her ideas that could help Liam, she then went to look inside the freezer to see if there was something she could take out to thaw for barbecue tomorrow. It would be a Saturday, and no one was working so they would have all day organizing and enjoy at the same time barbecue moments with him.

She took a package of seasoned barbecue meat and put it in a plastic container to thaw inside the fridge. She found a pint of black cherry ice cream and took it out. "Would you want some ice cream? I found a pint in the freezer."

"Sure, why not. It's too early to sleep. Let's watch some news." He went to grab the remote, sat on the couch, and switched on the TV. "Come sit by me here- the ten o'clock news is on!"

She brought with her two cups, spoons, and a pint of ice cream. She pulled the center table in front, placed the stuff on it, and grabbed a canister of chocolate cookies she had baked a few days ago. "Try my cookies. They are good with the ice cream."

"I'll have to watch myself. It looks like you're out to fatten me up!" He said, his eyes smiling at her, looking pleased with her considerate ways. "You're really making good on all your promises to me. Don't bother to do much on my account. You know I'm not helpless- I've been domesticated in my ways!"

"I'm the little sister, but I take care of my big brother when he's here, so it's not really too much for me to look after you. I cook for myself, so I don't have to put in any extra effort. I should be the one thankful, not only giving me peace of mind by being here but also helping me financially, which I think your offer is too much!"

"You're young, you're only starting to build up your life, and I'll appreciate it if you will allow me to help you with your immediate needs. I'm much older and financially stable to even take care of a wife. That's why helping you would not even put a dent in my lifestyle!" Liam jokingly said, looking at her.

"Then I'll miss you when you take a wife and leave me!" Suzy quipped, showing gloom in her hazel eyes.

"Don't be silly! I'm not planning on getting married, not in the near future, either! I like living with you here, so don't even think of me going away!" He said, pulling her close to him as they sat there eating cookies and ice cream.

When Liam woke up that morning, he was glad Suzy came to her senses and asked him what he had wanted to do before, to live with her in their LA house as he lived in their SF house with Jasper when he was doing some business there. Now, at last, he felt at home! He came out to find Suzy already had the table ready for breakfast. "Good morning, Liam. Your coffee is brewed and ready, the omelet is just cooked, and the bread is still warm and crunchy! Shall we?"

"Oh, Sue, you're a darling. I feel like a king! Nobody looked after me the way you do, not only now but always when I was visiting with your brother! I feel I'm imposing on you, and please don't spoil me!"

"Nope, you should know that you have chores around here. Let me do mine, and you can do yours at your convenience. Deal? Okay?"

"Yes, ma'am! Here let me pour hot water for your decaf coffee, no sugar, a little milk!" He said and gave her the cup. "Isn't it fun playing house?" They both laughed at the joke!

"You remembered! Thank you! And I know yours- in the morning, you want it brewed, strong and black, but in the afternoon, a little lighter, and at night, a glass of warm milk!"

"For a little brat, you're sharp! It feels good to know our preferences! I'll know more as we move on! This breakfast is good, especially the omelet with lots of veggies and cheese!"

"You have a lot of work to do, so you need the energy. I'll provide you with a laundry basket, and you make sure it's in the laundry room by Friday morning. There's a board on the fridge's side for messages between us. Make sure you have the date when you write it and the expected date when you need the request done. Trash day is Monday at 8 am- that's not hard because we're already up by then. And whoever comes in first will collect the mail to prevent thieves from pilfering our mail. Dinner is at 7 pm; eat alone and no waiting for the late comer!"

"Yes, ma'am, understood! I reserve the right to prepare dinner when I'm home early or buy food to go! We're both working, so we better save our energy and be very practical in everything about household chores, don't you agree? May I call or text you for important matters?"

"Sure, agreed! Communication is an important tool in our lives!" She was glad to know she could call or text him once in a while. "I better do some chores, but please, after lunch, I mean after the barbecue in the backyard, I'd like to discuss the other changes I want to make in the bigger room."

"It's good as it is. What do you need to change? I'll move my things later tonight or tomorrow. I don't want to bother you anymore."

"No bother. Everything I do is done voluntarily and willingly, so don't feel obligated to return any favor. I'll do some cleaning up, so don't move until I say so."

"What are you planning to do? Aren't you busy with other things?" He was trying to know what activities she was most interested in.

"Let's go downstairs and check what we can retrieve from the storage room- we need to get the grill and the charcoal. I prefer good old-fashioned cooking over the electric grill. The meat is more tender, juicy, and tastier."

"I like that too! I'd like to mow the yard while you're busy with the barbecue. It's good you have the auto sprinkler running at night. It's going to be hotter tomorrow and no rain for a week!" Liam used to come on weekends to help her with her yard work, did his weekly laundry mostly in the evening time, and parked his Porsche inside the garage for security, especially when he was out of town. He came and went since he had a key to the house and had a room designated for his use to store his other belongings since he had no permanent place of his own. At times, if Suzy was home, she invited him to stay the night or stay the week if she was away visiting Jasper in San Francisco. So, Liam was rather familiar with the household. The neighbors saw him almost every day and knew him well.

"I know. I saw the forecast. That's the reason I don't use pots for my flowering plants anymore; it's better to plant them on the ground for deeper roots."

"You have green thumbs- you're a good gardener. Your plants are vibrant, lush, and prolific. The evening breeze carries the fragrance upstairs, and I like the smell- it's very refreshingly aromatic!"

"That's why I choose perennial fragrant flowering plants, because of the smell permeating the air, and I don't need to keep planting new ones every year. They keep coming back- way less expensive that way!" She was surprised to find Liam very interested in plants and domestic chores. She appreciated his help but could not bring herself to ask him to reconsider moving in on a permanent basis until recently. She felt very brazen to ask him to live with her now, where she declined before when Jasper suggested it. She decided to set aside her pride and asked him anyway!

They went to do their respective chores until it was almost noon and Liam prepared the grill with the charcoal, so Suzy could start grilling the meat. All the things they needed were already on the table, including the cooler. This was a common activity in this household- during fall and winter, they barbequed on the balcony upstairs to avoid the cold and rain.

"I'll take a quick shower to get rid of the dust and grass and be back to help you." And he disappeared. He came back after over ten minutes. "How may I help?"

"That was quick! I have the meat ready, grab the drinks, and we're ready to eat. Would you prefer the hot sauce or the milder one?" The salad was a mix of greens, chunky mangoes sprinkled with salt, diced tomatoes, cilantro, and green onions, complementing the taste of the spicy smoked barbecue.

"Sit down and eat, don't worry about me- I'll help myself. You're tired of doing a lot already, I want you to relax and take it easy. We have all day to savor the good barbecue and salad. Here's your ginger ale, and I'll grab a beer."

They started eating the barbecue, which was really tender and tasty, because of the old-fashioned way of barbecuing. They continued talking and planning the rest of the day, enjoying the camaraderie. For the first time, Suzy was glad, very relaxed, and felt the joy of Liam's company which she had ignored and avoided in the past, afraid to get any closer to him that might expose her true feelings for him. But now, she decided to push aside her qualms and false pride and be as friendly to him as possible. He knew from the start she was attracted to him but tried her best to live with it and referred to it as a silly girlish preoccupation, which of course was not, but instead had grown into a budding genuine love for him. She was never interested in anyone. Although she made a few male friends, but never considered any admirer to ever win her heart because it belonged to Liam, then and now. It was just a crush in her childhood!

While eating, her mind drifted to other things like his most recent debacle of wooing Jasmine. Liam maintained his sense of dignity despite the failure, and he had not changed his good-natured attitude. Least of all, self-pity had no place in his heart- he remained calm, friendly, and engaging, most of all to Suzy and Jasmine, who were so close to each other that they were, practically, sisters. Suzy was sad about what transpired between Jasmine and Liam. When she played them for a possible match-up, she was greatly affected by the failure of that feat, regretting the fate of it. She did not mean to cause any discomfiture to Liam or imbue guilt on Jasmine. She unselfishly thought it was noble to want Liam to find happiness in spite of losing her chance to win him for herself. His happiness meant more than her own!

"Sue, you look so many miles away. What's on your mind? I'd like to help you find answers to whatever is cluttering your pretty head. I'd rather monopolize your attention," Liam said.

"Liam, I'm so sorry about you and Jasmine. I never intended to make you unhappy; I thought Jasmine was ready to give herself another chance at love. But it so happened that Zach stepped up to the plate to claim his place in Jasmine's heart when he learned about your pursuit."

"Don't beat yourself up for that nonsense. I believe things happen for a reason. There is a more pressing important thing to happen in my life, and that's what I should concentrate on and not cry over spilt milk! Do not apologize. In fact, I should thank you for making me realize who I'm really missing in my life instead of pursuing someone new."

"You are eyeing another damsel? Really? Whoa, you're fast and furious! I'm learning a lot about you!" She smiled at him, and her spirit lifted, knowing Liam was not hurting. "I would like to know who the new damsel is!"

"You would surely know it. A lot of things would blow you away with mixed emotions!" He said laughingly and teasing her.

"Such as? Tell me, or I'll tickle you to death!" She threatened him but with glee in her beautiful gleaming hazel eyes.

"I'd love that. Come do it, so I can chastise you, put you across my lap and make you learn not to tease or dare me, or you're going to get it!" He was nodding and signaling her to do as she had threatened. "Be brave, don't back down now!"

"Nah, you're the macho guy, and I'm just a small fry, chicken feed! I can't compete with you!" And they both laughed about it when they were caught up, even matched, and nowhere to go! They found they truly enjoyed each other, and Suzy was becoming comfortable kidding with him but still shy to confront his eyes when he contemplated her. She was afraid to give away her own feelings, her bottled love for him!

It was past three o'clock when they decided to clear up as the afternoon sun was getting hotter and the humidity was unbearable. Suzy took care of the leftover food while Liam helped in cleaning up. They went upstairs and switched on the aircon to cool the house. Liam said, "Time to take a nap! The warmth of the sun made me sleepy while the coolness inside the house is very welcoming," so he laid down on the couch by the den. Suzy sat by on the nearby reclining chair and put up her feet to relax. "You want to trade places. You can take the couch here," he offered.

Suzy declined, "Nope, it's more comfortable here, thanks." It was past 7 o'clock when both woke up after a restful afternoon. The sun was still out and did not get dark until about 10 o'clock at night at the height of summer.

Liam asked, "What now? I'm still full. Let's watch the news and find out what's happening around us." He went to the TV and switched it on. They sat comfortably next to each other. Liam was getting aware of the nearness of Suzy, whom he found to be sweet, straightforward, unsophisticated, and refreshingly awesome in her overall take on life. She was young and vibrant but a bit shy when teased or when attention was solidly directed at her. She was honest, hardworking with a down-to-earth, unpretentious attitude, and her congeniality was overwhelmingly contagious!

It crossed his mind how uplifting and simple it was to be sitting with her and giving him the pleasantness he had never experienced with anybody he had known. He told himself that this was the kind of domesticity he wanted in life.

He once in a while glanced at her youthful demeanor, which was so refreshingly awesome. He had never looked at her in the same light before, how appealing and attractive she was. He remembered what Jasper told him on her eighteenth birthday, "If you ever find my little sister, who has a tremendous crush on you, very appealing now, it's time to woo her, love knows no barrier, don't ever have any second thought. You have my blessings. You are better off than anybody else, and I know you'll take good care of her!" Liam promised Jasper he would look after her. That was why he stayed with her every now and then, to find the right moment and the chance to tell her about his love for her and about Jasper's blessings.

Looking at her now, he thought of the feasibility of confessing his love, not because she needed him, but because he was getting restless and conscious of her wonderful personality, her awesomeness, her nearness stirring masculine desire in him. He knew she had feelings for him from a long ago, and that was why she was evasive in looking directly to meet his countenance. He stirred, reclined his head on the couch, and looked up- his thoughts all caught up.

"What are you thinking about?" Suzy asked, giving him a side glance, waiting and anticipating his response.

"About a new budding consciousness of someone stirring my imaginations!" He said, lifting his head and looking at her.

"Wow, that's something very profound!" She looked at him and asked, "Do I know the damsel stirring your imaginations?"

He straightened out, "Sue, do you have someone special who's always in your mind, causes your heart to flutter, making you conscious of his nearness? How does it affect you? Tell me about your feelings, your dreams, your hopes, and wants in life!"

"Hold on, why are you asking me? Aren't we talking about you, someone whose nearness is stirring your imaginations? Not mine! Okay, first, you tell me yours, and then maybe I'll tell you mine. Deal?" Boldly, she dared him.

"Okay, but I want honesty, no bull. Or I'll punish you, and you have no way of escaping. I'm stronger than you are!"

"I know. You're the enforcer! Shoot, you go first."

"I'm realizing many things around me. I'm no longer looking at beautiful girls- I'm getting mellow and just observant. I'm looking at love in a different light, taking into account values and practical and important things in life. Stability of relationship, compatibility and sensibility, simple and refreshing beauty, compassion and trustworthiness, and chemistry, the magic of nearness."

"Gee, where would you find all these? Is there someone who would even have a bit of those qualities? If you can't find her, then you'll never marry?"

"Let me worry about where I can find her, and when I make my commitment known, I'll get married. Now it's your turn to tell me about your dreams, your wants, and desires, everything about him who moves your heart."

"Of course, I am in love with him, but he has to love me too. He's tall, educated, and very handsome! Nowhere he would consider me or, for that matter, even look at me in that light, since I'm not worth looking at, part and foremost of the desperation!"

"I'm tall, educated, and at least have been referred to as handsome, so am I that person you liked and loved? I asked you to count down what makes him tick, not describe his looks. A lot of guys have the three qualities you described. And don't put yourself down. It's not for you to say how guys feel about and see you."

She sat comfortably and stared at the wall and, in a dreamy way, said, "he's very lovable, kind, and accommodating- very considerate, always perceptive, solicitous of my needs, tender, and he looked at me like he wanted to take good care of me. He is the epitome of a family man, a conscientious, respectable being who sees the beauty and inherent goodness in every human being. He is simple in his ways and devoid of the brashness common in successful people. I would give it the world if only he cared for me even a little bit!"

"Really, Sue, are you truly in love? Come here. I thought you were young and carefree- I did not know how serious you look at human relationships. You are now a grown-up, a cut above your youth!" He pulled her close to him and looked at her beautiful hazel eyes. "If I were the object of such love, I would feel the happiest! Tell me who this guy is!" Although he knew Suzy was describing him, he feigned not knowing the guy who captured her heart.

Suzy came close, hugging him, exasperated for not guessing he was the one she was in love with! "Oh, well, he'll learn of my poor little self, being so much in love with him! Someday, maybe!"

"We both are in love, but we'll find our ways to their hearts, and in the meantime, we'll keep on loving them in our hearts and minds." He said and kissed her forehead, her scent made him aware of the wonder of her nearness, and he was bordering on taking her and kissing her as passionately as can possibly be!

The following day Liam had some appointments and was away most of the day. It gave time for Suzy to finish organizing the big room. She called on Nelson, the maintenance guy at their office, and two of his helpers to work scrubbing and sanding the floor, repainting the room a new color, washing the windows, laying the big carpet, and vacuuming it. The big mattress, the heavy couch, the Lazy Boy, drawers, and two long tables were moved from downstairs to the big room. By the afternoon, the setup was done completely. She sprayed the Air Wick freshener and kept the ceiling fan working to dry the paint and remove stale odor from the room, which had been closed for quite a long time.

It was six o'clock in the afternoon, and Suzy was about to finish cleaning the cabinets when Liam came home. "Sue, where are you?" He saw the door to the big room was open and assumed she was there. He could not believe his eyes when he saw the wonder she did to the room, all set and ready for occupancy! "Don't tell me you did all of this. You're not Samson to do all the moving of the heavy furniture. This is unbelievable. Where is your magic wand?"

He looked around, the new paint, the bed was made with the mattress covered with blue beddings, the heavy curtains were hung on both sides, with a flimsy beige curtain in the middle, floor sanded and varnished shine, the carpet was laid in the middle, and the cushion and throw pillows arranged by the bay window. The tables were full of all his drawings laid on top, and an office desk with two slim chairs was by the corner. Two sturdy lamp shades provided lighting. "You did all these? I can't believe how fast and efficient you are!"

"Move in tonight, and you can sleep here. Even your bathroom is also ready to use. You can hook up your computer, and if you want a landline, there is an outlet. You can have your television here at the foot of the bed. I did not ask them to bring up the old TV, it's too heavy, and I'm afraid it's no longer working. I had help- I called on our maintenance guy who did the work! I'm glad you like it!"

"Like it? I love it! You're a real darling! I don't know what to say- I'm much too impressed! Come here." He hugged her and kissed her and lifted her, swirling her twice! "Stay with me while I hook up all the electronics, you can help me move my clothes, and you can arrange them in the drawers. I like your way of doing things. I'll hang the heavy ones."

"Sure, I can do that, but don't you want to eat first? I made soup, and we have crunchy Italian bread. We have all the time- take it slow, enjoy the move."

"Anything you say sounds good to me. Okay, let's eat and tell me how your day was spent and all the things you did."

After dinner, they started filling up the big room; they went back and forth from the small to the big room moving everything. "Don't bother cleaning up. That's my chore. I'll do that tomorrow, or when I'm not busy, I'll convert that to a guest room or to house some of my hobby materials." Suzy decided what to do with the old room.

In between, they would sit on the bed, then Suzy lay down and contemplate the ceiling. Liam was watching her and was tempted to lie next to her. He asked, "What are you thinking now? Share it with me. I love to live in your head!"

"Nothing, it's a big bed- I'm lost in it, but when you had lain and joined me, it was just okay for two because you're a big guy!"

"Is there something wrong with that, being big?" He lifted his head, lay on his side facing Suzy, and looking at her tenderly, Suzy became conscious and wanted to get up and avoid his gaze. Liam held her arm to prevent her from leaving, "Stay, please. I want you here, at least for a while- I want to look at you, imagining the work you're capable of doing, thinking of the wonder of you!"

She smiled and stayed, Liam still holding her arm. She did not move and felt the warmth of Liam's nearness. She closed her eyes and wanted to stay there with him. Liam straightened and lay flat on his back, still holding hands with Suzy and applying pressure on her palm, squeezing it and looking at her. It was a very tender moment they shared and appreciated until Suzy got up and said, "Okay, break time is finished, back to work." He stopped her.

"Sue, I like you a lot. Lately, I've been thinking a lot about you; we're very similar in likes and wants in life, compatible in so many ways, and we share the same work and undertaking. We understand each other, I've grown accustomed to your ways, and I'm grateful for all the things you do for me. I'd been thinking, is there a chance to fit into the man of your dreams that you aptly described?"

She looked at him tenderly and said softly, "You're more than anyone could ever dream of, Liam, but I don't think I'm a good match for you. Love is attraction, and it is naturally born, a moving force that propels desire- a tingle that can only be satisfied by a collision of two minds and two hearts, a chemistry that's a mix of satisfaction from the innate and same attraction. I know love can also grow from mutual respect and out of the goodness of the heart. However, the first is truly arduous, hot, and passionate, while the latter is tender, kind, and warm. What kind of love can you offer me, Liam?"

"What kind of love do you want, Sue?" He softly whispered and looked at her sweetly and compassionately. "I'm capable of giving you both kinds!"

"I don't know, Liam, but I'm glad that you're offering me both. Do I want something born naturally, like love at first sight, fiery and compelling, or the kind of love that unfolds and evolves gradually from the goodness of one's heart and develops into something warm, encompassing, and tender? Or a love born out of pity because of my desolation?"

"You're never desolate, nor to be pitied, you're extraordinary, you're an exquisite species of a woman! Any man would be considered honored and privileged to be by your side! I would crave that honor, Sue, if you let me show you if you let me love you!"

She sat up and held her head with her both hands. It was too much for her to hear those words from Liam. Her tears fell, and she sobbed quietly.

Liam sat next beside her, held her shoulders tenderly, and begged, "Please don't cry. It's painful to see you like this, sad and hurt. Is it because I confessed that I've been confronted with my bottled feelings for you? But now that we've become closer and more acquainted, I thought you should know that I've been harboring this love long before you became friendly to me, during the days when you were mean and ignoring me. Jasper knew how I felt for you. Actually, he encouraged me to come clean and start wooing you."

She could not believe what he was telling her. She thought it was just to appease her sadness and because she had done a lot of work to accommodate him. "Will you excuse me- this is too much. If you don't mind, let's talk about this some other time? I'm much too overwhelmed."

"My conscience would not let me sleep. Stay with me for a while until you're pacified and calm. I can't let you out of sight, knowing I caused this turmoil in your mind." He guided her, and they sat on the couch, his hand around her shoulders, her head on the nook of his, and said, "Please lay your head on my shoulders, don't think of anything, just rest." She did not know how long they were in that position, his other hand holding hers. The sweetness of being near penetrated deep into their core and intoxicated them!

When she felt better, she sat up straight and told Liam she had calmed down and was getting sleepy. She bid him good night, but Liam stopped and asked her if she was all right. "I am all right, Liam, don't worry about me. I'm a big girl now. I'll see you tomorrow bright and early," and she even tiptoed and kissed him, barely reaching his chin- that was how far she could reach him, being tall.

He returned her kiss, tenderly brushed his lips on her cheeks, and said, "Good night, sweet dreams, remember I love you, not because you had a crush on me since you were twelve!" He would not let go of her hand while at the door, and before she disappeared, she turned and asked.

"Who could have told you that? You were not as good-looking as you're now! I knew Jasper told you, but he was only trying to get even with me because I discovered his letter to one of your classmates!"

"Because he saw me watching you earnestly on your eighteenth birthday celebration and teased me about my unspoken love for you. He actually encouraged me to return your love since the feeling was mutual. He told me he would rather see you with me than with any of your admirers!"

"Did he really say that? You guys are ganging up on me!" A little embarrassed but happy to have known Liam got conscious about her since she was eighteen! She gave him a knowing fleeting glance before she closed the door behind her.

She was tired from what she worked on yesterday preparing the big room for Liam and terribly exhausted emotionally about the revelations and admissions of guilt on mutually pining for each other in an unspoken way. It was a long time coming. Her love for him started a decade ago when she was twelve up to now- at the age of twenty-two!

She overslept and could not bring herself to get up and meet the scrutinizing gazes of Liam, revealing her heart, soul, and body! She covered herself and buried her face in her pillow when she felt the weight of someone behind her.

"Wake up, little Sue. Your coffee is getting cold! He had lain next to her, behind her, his hand on her shoulder, caressing her tenderly. "Come, I made you some egg omelet and sizzling bacon for your breakfast!" He pulled the sheet to expose her face, kissed her cheek, and pulled her up to a sitting position.

"You did not have to do that out of gratitude for what I did for you preparing the big room." She could not look at him without baring her smitten feelings!

"I know you did a lot, but it's not because of that I made you breakfast. I really wanted to! I want to get closer to your heart so that you can see and feel what I had for you a long time ago! It was born naturally. The seed had grown and is now in full bloom to get noticed, ripe for you to pluck!" As he was explaining, his eyes were bathing in her morning glow, wanting to kiss her with unbridled passion and take her in his arms to bask in her freshness, to unleash the scorching heat that was incessantly burning inside him.

She straightened up and moved out of bed with Liam helping her, his nearness was battering her senses, and like him, she was consumed with the anticipation of the beauty, passion, and ecstasy of love awakening after lying dormant for quite a long time! She went to the bathroom to freshen up, to hide the raw emotions from Liam, who was on a constant watch, reading all the littlest vibes he could sense.

Liam was still there in wait for her, primly walked her to the breakfast counter and served her deluxe style! She was not used to any service but was delighted that Liam was really paying attention to her, even though she would prefer to be the one giving the service. As mischievously as he could, Liam understood her predicament at the moment, had that knowing smile, and welcomed the idea of getting the best service from her in *another* way!

"I think by now, I can decipher that look in your eyes, knowing you are as being mischievous as you can be. You're interpreting things in a different light." She said, her lips tightly set!

"Care to elaborate? I will expunge whatever you deduce wrong and remember the consequence you get from every wrong concept or guess! At my command, you would be chastised, and you have no choice or vote on how I desire to unleash it, bit by bit! Where, when, and how, not your decision but mine!"

"Okay, it looks like it's a strip game, I surmise, seeing that devilish dark mischief playing on your expressive petulant eyes while your lustful tempestuous lips, almost savoring what your snarling dirty mind is perversely brewing!"

"Wow, that's a handful of unsavory descriptions, very profound! I think I'm incapable of those. Don't I deserve a little bit of accolade? I did not know that I'm the one with a mean streak, unappreciated, thus deemed unworthy of your love and respect, care and affection! Poor me!"

"Really, it's not meant that way! Sorry, what I want to say is, that you're very confident you can get your way with me, too sexy and sensual to be ignored, much too arduous to sustain your amorous forte, truly unstoppable to get what you want, and mighty anxious to reap your reward! In short, I'm overwhelmed, left with no choice but to succumb to your strength and unrelenting charisma!"

"Okay, if you put it that way, that's quite an elation! But can't you see, I have to be firm with you to get what I want, to make you see and feel what I can give, and what I can offer in a lifetime? I want you to share my warmth, feel my touch, enjoy my nearness, and get all the love and comfort of my arms! With a good challenge, winning our game is the only way I can get my hands on you! Have you even begun to comprehend that? No way, you'll come to me without a fight, no matter how unsuspectingly my ploy is! You'll never give me a loving, sweet surrender unless I coerce you! You're wise, a sharpshooter who would not shy away from a challenge! And that's commendable of you but unsavory for me!"

"Why you have designs on me, that's something to ponder, Liam? I'm bashful to even look at you, and maybe your way would teach me to respond in ways more than I could ever imagine! Thanks for the considerate plan to make me feel your presence, to tickle the imagination to stir something sensual! Very natural to your carnal concept, maybe none other?"

"Stop interpreting my motives! Look at me, Sue, lock eyes with me, know what's in my soul, what and how I feel about you. God knows how I want to make love to you! I truly want to know you- your body and your soul. Will you let me in, open your heart for me? I need you to come to terms with that! Make you aware of your own feelings, what the nearness of me does, what my love means, if we are ready to contemplate a life together!"

"I think I can do that, but be patient with me, Liam. I have never been anywhere near what you're offering me now." She dared, for the first time, to look at him in the way she had always wanted to do, full of love, without hesitance or any reservation! Shedding doubts, apprehension, and impertinence totally!

"Yes, Sue, your wish is my command. I'll patiently teach you everything about relationships, for both our sake and need!" He went around the counter, pulled her up, and gave her the first passionate kiss he had longed desired for quite some time now! It was tender, probing, wet and long; it made them hungry and wild, a new passion born between them. Catching his breath, he let go and said, "Finish your food, and we have a lot to do in the big room!"

He got busy assembling his computer when he heard the phone ringing in the dining room. He listened to Suzy talking, and it was not Jasper! He walked out to check on Suzy.

Suzy covered the mouthpiece, walked towards him, and mouthed, "Jasmine." Liam nodded and returned to what he was doing inside his room, followed by Suzy, sitting where Liam could hear her conversation with Jasmine.

"It's been a while since we have talked. Why not come here to enjoy another good pizza time! Oh, a scoop! Don't be surprised- I finally made Liam move in with me! I asked him, actually begged him," she stopped to wink at Liam and gave him a thumbs-up gesture, continued talking, "he's been wasting his time hopping from one hotel to another when this house is big and empty! Besides, Jasper has been so busy and doesn't visit often anymore. For security reasons, you know, and what you had suggested."

Hearing that, Liam stopped working and paid attention to the conversation, interested in what Jasmine suggested to Suzy, and hearing her talk about him, who bounced the idea of coming clean about her feelings for Liam.

"You are getting sensible. There are a lot of advantages, and you know that. Forget about your stubborn streak- he's a great guy for the taking! If I were you, I'd put a collar on him, stake a claim, chain him and never let him go; he's not only kind and very respectful but unapologetically handsome! Wow, where in the world could you ever find such a combination!" Jasmine told Suzy, "And don't let Julie come anywhere near him!" Jasmine laughed, a bellow. It was not meant for Zach to hear the joke! Good thing he was not around!

"Yeah, yeah, you're always right! So, when are you coming this weekend? I'll get the pizza- that's easy! Looking forward to it, I've got a lot of things on my mind!" She hung up and looked at Liam, who was waiting to be apprised of what were the suggestions Jasmine gave her.

"Give it to me- you ladies have a way of making fun and light of any situation. At least let me know what those beautiful heads can concoct!" Liam opined. "Amuse me!"

"She thought Zach did not care for her, and she was miserable. So, I advised her it was time for her to find new love, and to help out, I introduced you to her. *'Since I can't have you, why not offer you to a friend!'* A few days after you guys met, Zach proposed, and she accepted after a long decade of waiting. We talked right after their engagement, and she found out I was lamenting my unrequited love, an over a decade crush I had on you! I told her it would never materialize since you saw me like a little sister instead of a possible love interest."

She continued on, "Jasmine wondered and asked me why did I offer you to her as a possible new love interest? Well, I said if you couldn't be mine, she might as well have you instead of falling into the hands of she-devils who would really, no doubt, chase you!"

A bit embarrassed for wanting him, she confirmed what was in Liam's mind about her unspoken love. "Jasmine, understanding my desolation about your lack of interest in me, said it's better to get closer to you- saying you deserve someone who truly cares. Someone, you know, instead of you looking elsewhere, ending into the hands of what she calls 'she-devils' lurking in your midst!" Suzy earnestly admitted.

"I liked Jasmine because you painted a very well-balanced person with beauty in and out. I tried your plan to get closer to her, but her heart was already taken by Zach, who had known her since a decade ago. I understood that. Anyway, at that same time, I was wary of you for truly loving me. I thought I was too old and very conservative for you, and we were moving in different circles, in spite of Jasper's advice and blessings!" Liam was not sure then whether it was wise to snatch her from the cradle, so to speak!

"We only have a six-year difference in age- that's nothing compared to the 25 or 35-year difference between women marrying older men. It's society's trend!"

"Not for me! Too much age difference could spell disaster. There would be lots of disagreements, losing any chance of compatibility, not to mention peace and quiet in life! Yes, like you said, our gap is only six, but you seem to be wiser and more stable than anybody I know in your age bracket! And now, my heart can't afford to lose the love and good chemistry we have! That is why it's timely to snatch you from the cradle and never let go!"

He approached her, on the one hand, held her chin, brushed his lips against hers, softly and convincingly, he said in his velvety voice, "Let you and me get together, do with some of the possibilities of a very memorable interlude, that would eventually capitulate into a very impassioned pleasure!" The invitation was sensual, enticing, and sexy!

"At your beck and call," she consented, quickly and unwittingly, without digesting the implications! Would she really? Was it a quip or not? Hadn't she broken the laws of chances lately, once too often, for such another ingenious love adventure with Liam? Had she strayed farther than most lost souls when it came to the lure of the flesh? With Liam, she had the propensity for that sort of muddle. She could not walk it off, to sashay out of his room after she had committed to what she said. She had to suffer the consequence, as Liam had arrogantly put it!

It ain't easy to play with fire, to goad or spur with words when you're on the short end of the stick, and his prize not viable at the moment, although pertinent but not yet, to be on hold possibly until she had mustered enough courage to deal with him on a very personal and intimate level!

In the meantime, she had to dally away, but she knew the consequence of that altogether! He warned her not to come hot on the heels to ambush, buck or parry from the logical end of an inference! Her avowal sounded eager, submissive, and yet, he couldn't be totally sure. She was elusive and very smart- she had mastered the cat and mouse game! Liam was the opposite of a surly bloke; would he act like one to get to her?

Suzy was neither pensive nor excited. A morsel of humility would help her unwind. Contemplative of Liam, he was throbbing with anticipation, the pleasure of getting a trophy at her expense- it neither soothed her regrets nor averted her impending doom. She writhed in uncalled-for shame when she missed the mark and walked right straight where Liam wanted her to be, at his mercy! It was a faux pas on her side! Liam, none other, was her nemesis! To plan a side step was useless, a waste of precious time, but nonetheless, worth thinking about to avert Liam's designs for a caper, an extravagant interlude that could end in an exhausting encounter! It could also mean a splendid memorable experience worth remembering, a dawning of herself!

Liam became busy for the whole week on a project. A new client, who was involved in purchasing and developing a huge gated community in the northern outskirt of the city proper, made various selections from Liam's collection of Architectural Designs for residential homes. He was working late compiling the chosen plans and working hand in hand coordinating with Jasper about possible builders from San Francisco and Los Angeles, both of them preoccupied with their respective expertise!

It threw off Liam's pursuit of Suzy, a respite from his quest for intimacy and amorous inclinations. On the other hand, Suzy was glad to have the kind of tranquility for an indefinite period while quietly ignoring Liam's persistent and demanding grit. After a hard day's work, he wanted relaxation with the quiet enjoyment of Suzy's company. He was incessantly toying with the idea that Suzy would sleep with him in the big room to get truly acquainted in bed. Suzy was trying hard to delay the inevitable; she knew sooner or later, Liam would press her, and she had no strength to refuse. After all, she unequivocally promised that to him, and she should not back down from that! Keep her word, so to speak!

It was Saturday afternoon when Jasmine paid a visit, and they had pizza and other finger food plus drinks and beer. Liam went to his office to meet his client, and he did not know whether he could be back to catch up on Jasmine. The two women had the time to talk personally about their love life and the demanding romantic encounters of their relationship. There were no doubts as to the integrity and trust of the men they were involved with; their concern was the intensity of the demands that were put on them, that of living like husband and wife since they both lived with their lovers! That was the part they wanted to negotiate, but that was moot! The quality time was never for themselves but for sharing with their beloved men!

There was no irony, that kind of life was better than without the love they had long waited for. Both waited a decade for their **unrequited love** to be returned, rewarded! In contemplation, their choice would be by their side, being loved, and to make their lovers feel truly ingratiate!

Liam came home a bit later than he expected, supper would soon be ready, but it was still bright outside. He went straight to Suzy and tapped the half-opened door, but the TV was on. Suzy did not hear the slight knocking. She had just come out of the shower- her half-dried, wavy tresses touching the length of her shoulders, a pink towel wrapped around hugging the soft contour of her supple body, a vision of wholesome freshness! She moved to pick up the TV remote when her towel dropped to the floor, exposing the fair softness of womanliness, genuine and pure, untouched by any adulteration, stark naked before his eyes, beholding her in awe!

He could not help but approach her, "Sue, you're so beautiful! Stop, don't move- let me just behold and fill my eyes with your awesomeness! Let me hold you, feel your softness, and smell your freshness. You're amazing!"

Suzy, stunned, stayed put, caviling the desire to hide her nudity while Liam approached, his eyes probing her body in sheer delight, observing her with an indulgent expression, bathing in the beauty of her nude body, so exquisite, so extremely sensual sending thunderbolts of desire all over him, shocks and waves of seared awareness, he wanted his hands to touch, to caress her and totally get lost in her glory and splendor!

"I want you, now, completely. I can't, and I won't let go; you're mine! Don't say no- please let me love you!" Speaking incoherently, overwhelmed with rapturous sensuality, with graceful reverence, he scooped her body, walked and took her to his room, and gently laid her on the bed. With great haste, he nimbly took off his clothes and joined her! He felt like a trapped animal, his desire exploding, eager to contain the scorching heat of passion burning inside of him, with a blazing sensation overwhelming him, emboldening, craving for release and gratification, his antidote to insanity!

Suzy, herself, was a helpless prey of emotional awakening. Hers was young, fresh, wild, and untamed, moving to a highly sensuous state, wantonly inviting, in wait for the heavenly and ultimate bliss promised by Liam's love! He was kissing her ardently, gently touching, inviting her with impassioned persuasion to his lovemaking. He started slow, enticingly sweet and tender, intense and passionate, releasing the burning desire that made him relentless, peaked to a fierce, almost savage, undeniably unapologetic at its height, where he rapturously took her innocence amidst the ecstasy and rapture, ending in their climactic coming in unison!

After an almost eternity of bliss, they had lain there in a calm, sweet embrace, their spent and exhausted bodies fully satiated! They did not move, savoring the full satisfaction of the wonder of their love encounter! It was their first! And possibly, the fieriest and most memorable one in their life together!

Still in ecstatic mode but fully aware, Liam moved and reached for the side bed drawer, took out a red velvet box, sat on the bed, and said, "Sue, my sweet love, open your eyes," and when Suzy opened her eyes, she heard Liam saying, "I love you, then and now. Will you marry me?" His hand holding the box, his lips with a quiver, his eyes imploring, waiting in great anticipation for her response!

Suzy sat up in quaint amazement to meet Liam's tender gaze, looked at the ring, and in the sweetest way, she softly uttered, "Yes, Liam, you're my one and only love- I will marry you. You made me the happiest; I've long dreamt of hearing your words from the day we crossed paths on our doorsteps twelve years ago!" She moved to close the gap between them to give Liam the sweetest kiss on her quivering lips. Liam took her lips and sealed the covenant of love!

After the loving kisses, Liam picked up his cell phone by the side table, pulled Suzy next to him, the bed sheet over themselves, and took some pictures for posterity to record their engagement. They laughed at the instance that it was taken, nudity in hiding!

Liam, fully awakened, having been sensually exalted and satisfied, went to the kitchen and checked what dinner he could serve Suzy! The spicy stew was hot from the slow cooker, and with a small crunchy morsel of bread, he served

Suzy an appetizing dinner in bed, to her surprise and gratitude! "Wow, this is really an outrageous service deluxe, after all the loving delights! Do I really deserve this?"

"More than I could ever want to give you, more than you deserve to have, in appreciation of the wonderful heretofore satisfaction you've shared with me unselfishly, with unprecedented reverence!"

Suzy felt the depth and breadth of Liam's values, his dignified view of life, the measure of the quality of his love and integrity! She was lucky to have loved such a kind of a man Liam was! Now she understood what he was all about; Jasmine's perception of his character aptly suited him, and his sensuality ran deep in his veins!

When Jasmine came home late in the afternoon, she found Zach already preparing dinner, greeted him with enthusiasm, kissing him eagerly, missing the closeness they had come to find in their cohabitation of late! "Hmm, that's a sweet, sensuous kiss from you I've never experienced before! What gives, my mate?" Zach enticingly deepened the kiss, beholding, teasing her with ardent, sensual groping of her soft curves. He was encouraging her to ceremoniously strip tease, his piquancy to whet his appetite for sensual foreplay that would later culminate in a torrid sexual encounter to satiate their quest for ecstasy and gratification!

She looked at him with her half-opened mouth, inviting Zach to explore the heat she was feeling at the moment. He capitulated, his own insatiable fiery virility unleashing, deeply compelled to quash the escaping heat from his core, his muscled thighs rubbing and molding against the softness of her body. His face, with chiseled handsomeness, was in wanton languor to take her right there on the width of the dining table. Her exquisite beautiful body, stark naked, splayed before him, a panorama for his full beholding, he lingered, propelling his appetite while dwelling on her bold bareness for his taking, anytime! Jasmine was always complicit in the quest for the best that could heighten and satiate all their fantasies, from mundane to bold, undaunted, impetuous, and precipitous! The encounter always ended in an explosive climactic and glorious copulation!

After their laborious lovemaking, he took her limber and worn out soft bare body, tenderly laid her on the bed, covered her with a flimsy beige colored cloth, her full breast, and her womanhood partly draped, the beauty displayed was in its glorious splendor, his eyes could not stop gazing! He was basking, contemplating his favorite work of art, the inherent graceful splendor Jasmine was! And she was his! He wanted to take her again, be lost inside of her- he was under her spell, now and forever!

He lay next to her, his hand holding her tenderly, his eyes closed, savoring the nearness, the satisfaction of feeling whole with Jasmine's presence in his life. Overwhelmed with those thoughts and feelings, he wanted to marry her as soon as possible!

Jasmine and Suzy met a few years back when they worked for the same company. They became close, sharing almost similar love-life stories- loving someone dearly, not knowing if their love would and could ever find any realization! Both languished in the loneliness of an unrequited kind of love but were in good faith that someday, somehow, they could find happiness in their love life. There were twists and turns that happened, and their lives became intertwined with the objects of their affection, and with the solemn promise and firmness of purpose, they went out to find love. They continued and ventured in life until both found that love was a mystery and would find its way to those who truly believed!

After a decade of a journey, Zach realized that Jasmine was the one he had truly loved and was ready to take his life to the level where he could give all that he had to offer matrimony to Jasmine, who had waited long enough! In the same light, Liam had known Suzy since she was twelve, knew of her unspoken love for him, now having his own love for her unleashed, awakened to consciousness, and after tasting and reaping her innocence, he gave her an engagement ring and basking in her awesome youthful freshness, he would like to take her to the realm of matrimony so that they could start a family!

Both the women, Jasmine and Suzy, the object of love, found, returned, conquered, satisfied, and worthy of keeping, were now the wooed brides on the outcoming marriage celebration by the prospective grooms, Zach and Liam.

When their lovers told them to pick a date when they would like to take their vows and where to hold the wedding, Jasmine and Suzy were ecstatic and shared their joy! They wanted a double wedding; they were friends, who found love because they waited patiently, had faith in the wisdom of God, and glibly believed in the adage 'love knows no barrier' it seeks where its groove fits well!

The Cathedral in the city proper was the choice- it was well decorated with all kinds of white, blue, and fragrant pink flowers, glittering silk bias of white lace connecting the pews on the aisle side. A red carpet lain started at the steps of the church ending before the steps to the altar, candlelight of various sizes scattered around to give the desired lighting. An organ playing the soft bridal music was next to the oversized wedding trellis covered by white satin, the top crowned with white roses, and on the side, trails of blue-violet and white wisteria hanged loosely! The chairs for the brides and grooms were fully covered with white velvet.

At the sound of the organ playing the wedding march, the bridal entourage came walking down the aisle, two by two, dispersing at the altar to their respective places where the grooms were on each side. The elegant, ravishing brides had each exquisite bouquet in one hand, holding hand on the other, demurely marched down and were met by their respective beloved grooms. It was a fateful day, solemn and memorable. Each couple recited their vows, rings were exchanged, they were joined in matrimony by the Cardinal who blessed them, and thus each couple was pronounced husband and wife! The two couples kissed, each groom taking his bride, sealing their marriage with a sweet, tender, and passionate kiss to the joy of all the family, friends, and acquaintances! Lots of pictures were taken for posterity!

The reception followed at the Italian Restaurant where they served sumptuous Italian and American cuisine, and then the merriment started, grooms and brides dancing, joined by the entourage with the rest enjoying the celebration!

Before the celebration ended, the couples left for their trips to their respective choice of destinations for their honeymoon! Congratulations to the newlyweds were offered by family, friends, and relations!

Zach and Jasmine, after their honeymoon in the Bahamas went back to the usual computer data processing business, most of the time, they drove together, but when Zach found time to check on his old household since Julie was still there, he took his own car, it gave Jasmine time to do her grocery shopping and a little time to herself, Zach at least spending one night with Julie to find out all the needs in the house. He scheduled this one night, especially on a Friday, to give him the whole Saturday to resolve all issues. It was all right with Jasmine for Zach to be away twice a month. At times she spent the night with him there, helping out and having at least a connection with Julie, whom she found delightfully acceptable as a young sister-in-law. Jasmine completely discarded any jealousy. She knew how devotedly in love Zach was with her.

They told Julie to continue living there if she wished to, since her plans of going abroad had been postponed. She met and started going out with a friend, who was a new doctor. She met while she was working part-time at the hospital. She was thrilled to have found someone who had the rare qualities she found and admired in Zach. Jasmine and Zach were happy for her- her maturity was, perhaps, beyond her age!

While Liam's architectural business was at a fast pace, Suzy resigned from the computer company she worked for to dedicate her organizational capabilities as the manager/secretary to Liam. His partnership business with Jasper was also very successful and booming; therefore, Suzy was needed by their partnership too. She was on top of everything. She was happy to be working for the two people she most cared for in the world. Liam, being very loving and protective of her, always took her with him anywhere he traveled, to the delight of Suzy, who was always at his beck and call, as she quite put it! To the delight of Jasmine and Suzy, their love was unrequited no more!

"If you believe in true love, you will find it. If love endures because of nurturing, with its wings spreading joy and happiness, it becomes the most beautiful thing in the world!" One should never lose faith in LOVE!

THE END

Made in the USA
Middletown, DE
04 August 2022

70426886R00149